The Miserable Jerk Collection

Daniel Olney

Cover art by Morgan DeLorenzo

This book is a work of fiction. All names, characters, places and incidents are, however, based on you.

Edited by Sarah Knobloch Olney

ISBN: 978-0-557-70117-9

www.lulu.com

Dedicated to Rebecca

Table of Contents

Proving to the Cat My Greatness

His heaving grey form sucks in all my air and methodically kicks it out again after letting it ricochet all throughout its fat body. Most of the day its eyes are closed and its curled up somewhere. Its eyes shut so tight it's fighting to keep them closed, concentrating to stay limp and euphoric and sleep away the universe.

There has never been any organism I've wanted to kick more then that cat. It's got such a cocky distrust of the waking world and the disdainful looks it shines on me don't help our relationship.

I'm trying my best to simulate the sublime state it rests in but he has an advantage I don't. No not the fur. He can fit on top of my cable box and just enjoy its heat, for an animal of that size it must be like the most impressive top of the line heated blanket. My cheap couch caresses me with decent cushioning but I'm not in the same space. I'm not practiced with the same level of contentment.

His tail falls off of the top of the box and covers the time making it impossible for me to change the channel while Keith Olbermann calls everyone he doesn't agree with names. He's that guy in line behind you spouting off to a friend seeming to hate everything and after a minute or two he makes you seriously think about hopping to a new line. I pop up off the couch, for a split second my robe opens revealing my black and colored Pac-Man boxer shorts. I'm reaching for a wrinkled used tissue, bunches of them lay on the ground next to me. With energy and exuberance only found in me when unhappy I snatch up three of them and use all my strength to hurl the first one at the cat. If only a tissue could cave in a skull in a way that wouldn't leak brains into my cable box. Cat brains ruin cable boxes.

"Get the fuck off…" Everything I say after that doesn't make any sense I learned it all from Elmer Fudd. It has great emotional meaning but not a direct translation into English. Tissues don't fly like baseballs, even when you reuse and reuse them until your mind assumes that it must be weighed down with enough snot to make it a reasonable weapon. After it left my fist I wanted it to beam over in a straight line and smack the stupid cat, that's how I pictured it. What I got was the flight of a child's first paper airplane, unsteady and going in no sensible direction. The cat doesn't even open its eye to note the effort.

It has a name but its name is stupid. She named it Bella. It's the name you give a female French assassin or a ballerina. It makes me feel like an idiot when I say it so I don't. I can't even mute his big angry red pundit face with the limp grey tail of Bella blocking it. This time I kick my legs off the couch leaning forward and with my second try I throw all my intensity into it. I put everything that makes me who I am, all the determination that got me where I am today into my left arm and somehow I find the strength.

I sunk your fucking battleship cat. It bounced right off his skull and I got to see that left ear tweak and his eyes pop open. The grey matted fur that lay so peaceful jumped up and my finger was never so determined. Click. I win.

Not that I'm going to find anything enlightening on another channel but I have degrees of sensitivity, I can take a hot shower but I'll burn in a hot stove. That's why I changed it to MTV Jams which is supposed to be their opportunity to take the M in their name back. The only way it resembles the old days of MTV is that they play the same seven videos again and again until you know every video vixen by blank stare. You just don't know their names.

The cat still hasn't forgiven me. I pulled my robe tight again and laid back into the cushions but his eyes are slits and his mouth is pulled so tight he looks like he wants to curse my mother.

"Cat she's not here. She'll cuddle you later."

Nothing. Still watching me.

"What!? I'm not like that. I save all my cuddling for her. I got nothing left for you."

Face unchanged, eyes still focused.

"You pay rent I'll cuddle the shit out of you."

For a while I try and ignore the cat and just watch the videos and figure out if Krump dancing is anything I care to understand. I have a tough time relating to cats, they know that I don't like them. Cats are smart enough to pick up on little things even when you're not cruel to them. I had a roommate who used to smush his cat's face in his own poo to let him know that he meant business. The cat never let him rest. It sought his personal space out as a poo target from then on and it never stopped until he eased up on him. I'm not even into that. I don't have the energy to be cruel to that miserable hairy freeloader; I just strive to co-exist until I outlive it.

Ignoring something is never the way to solve it. His face never changed not even an inch. His stare was boring a hole in me and so I decided to pay him back. I shut off the television, there goes the heated blanket.

"I don't know what I did to you. Just because I hate you doesn't mean you have to be immature and hate me back. Two wrongs don't make a right."

I get up from the couch and walk out into the kitchen from my living room seeking out the cheez-its cardboard exoskeleton. I pop its mouth open and tear its innards from it, grabbing what's left of the orange juice jug from the fridge on my way.

"You want to ruin my television experience you little bastard then I'm going to talk to you until your sick of me like everyone else. You'll wish you had just waited for her to get back."

Next to the tissues is a black laptop which I pull open and with a mighty stab I press the power button.

"You probably think you know a lot about humans. I know more then you. I've seen them through all the possible swings of fate and mood, and if your problem with me is that I haven't given you the sweet simple gestures of kindness that she has over the years I can resolve that. I'll do you one big kindness; I'll tell you about all of them at least the one's I've known. Maybe your disrespectful ass will learn to respect the fragile state of the human condition! Then you have to tell my why the Egyptians were stupid enough to think you were holy. "

The cat's eye seems to twitch.

"I will be taking breaks for breakfast."

It twitches again.

"I tell you when it's too late for breakfast, you fuck."

Of the Wise and the Drunk

I remember the day complete with each smell taste and sensation but I don't recall the date or even the year. Nothing in the world ever felt like opening Jose's freezer on a Friday night. To pull on the black handle and let the chilled streams of air dance on my face knowing without looking in, what would be inside? Our treasure chest.

It wasn't really Jose's freezer, to be precise none of us had any property due to the contractual obligation we signed we were ourselves property (in a literal sense) of the government. It was Jose's barracks but more importantly our gathering place. They were already gathered for the consecration of the evening when I came through the door, I didn't address them or even turn my eyes to them they were such a certainty. I pulled the door and took in the chunks of freezing air until my face acclimated to the sensation. I opened my eyes to what was inside. Johnny Walker Black label, Crown Royal, Remy Martin VSOP, Glennfiddich single malt scotch whiskey, and SOJU.

We kept them all in the freezer to chill the liquor as much as we could and of course on each side packages of chipped ice acted as bookends. I possessed no mixed emotions in this moment which is important. I could cover my back and acknowledge some sort of inner turmoil and worry that I was doing something bad to myself. I could expound and justify and belabor this point but at that moment no scene was more beautiful or true then that lineup with the deep brown texture of the Johnny Black and the bloated bottle with the strange golden cap on the Crown.

I heard the music playing as I walked in, it was from a CD I burned for everyone in our crew. That's all anyone did in Korea was run in a crew to protect the interests of the group. As I looked towards them Rose caught my attention first. None of us called him Rose that often because it was his real last name and much too normal for him. We called him Utah and he liked it or at least pretended too. This was a night like so many where he had spread his wiry frame and begun dancing all over the room on the cheap carpeting. That unmitigated Anglo smile coating his entire face and over the music (which was loud) I could hear the ice in his scotch bump shoulders in his glass. That's the art of drinking.

I pulled out a glass, diminutive but stout and sturdy easy to grip and move with. I again pulled at the black handle and sucked the streaming refrigeration into my nose, reaching out for the great bag of ice on the left of the bottles. As I undid it's top and dug into the chamber of ice Rose spoke.

"Where you been Dave? We had to start without you." His face was chipper and his body bounced as he finished every sound.

I dropped a platoon of ice chips into the glass and un-sheathed the Johnny Black before responding "Fucking Sergeant Rogers had me on some room inspection shit, had me waiting for an hour." He knew immediately of my plight and ongoing battle with Staff Sergeant Rogers of my own dear Water Platoon. He would walk by as he was getting out of formation and see the statuesque muscular figure of Staff Sergeant Rogers standing over me forcing me to do pushup after pushup. Rose just nodded and pretended to hold back a chuckle as Jose's voice sounded off from the bathroom through the door yelling. "FUCK THAT MOTHERFUCKER."

We burst with coordinated laughter. We had been meeting in Jose's barracks every night we were free from the extra work our duty station was so known for. When they called off the late night changing tires in the dark, driving around in circles expeditions we would gather here and discuss everything in depth. In dirty uniforms or double breasted suits we were there. The three wise men as we called ourselves, from a movie where Denzel Washington plays a corrupt cop and reports to three nameless old guys in nice suits that laugh nicely with him and warn him not to screw up. In the movie they were The Three Wise men with all the power and influence and tonight so were we.

The brown Johnny Black licked the edges of my glass and forced the ice to pop and crackle, pushing it upward as I poured. Once I was satisfied with the amount and the sound I moved toward an open chair. It was wood with a small cushion that didn't go far enough towards making it comfortable. Rose was in a chair of the same structure next to me with his smooth scotch and toothy grin we just started bobbing our head to Bone Thugs N' Harmony's FOR THE LOVE OF MONEY and chatting proudly about new people that joined the platoon, the women mostly. Jose and Rose's supply platoon always had the best run of attractive women and Rose was very happy to discuss it.

Jose came out of the bathroom fixed up with a red and white striped Ralph Lauren Polo shirt, tucked into starch stiffened creased khaki's. He was and still is very short and on that day he had spiked the front of his black hair with some kind of product. I knew that the SOJU in the freezer was his and was proven correct when he grabbed forcefully the same black handle and tore it from the liquor lineup (along with the ice).

SOJU is a very hard thing to describe to rational people. It's clear like vodka but that's where the comparison ends. A group of people can drink SOJU for hours because of the smooth affectionate greeting it has for you and continue to drink it while conversing, laughing and gesturing but when they stand up GOD WILL KICK THEM. Standing will spin them a hundred and sixty times around in circles until the world is destroyed at its very foundation. Our commander would routinely warn us not to drink SOJU but no one listened. It was everywhere here and real cheap all you had to do was mix it with something rich and you were gone. We all had had experiences and toned down our SOJU consumption, except for Jose.

There he was filling a larger glass with too much of the transparent stuff and mixing it with Boone's Farm which is an evil substance by itself. He spoke to us only after he took his first lustful sip of the mad creation.

"What the fuck you guy's talking about?" He looked around, darting seemingly black pupils at both of us.

"Utah says you look like John Leguizamo." I made up things for Rose to have said all the time to keep him involved.

Jose smiles and sits in the third chair, completing our triangulation but not before chocking the door open to watch the people as they pass, and solicit the girls by complimenting them on their beauty, enjoying them all dressed up and having left his wedding ring on the dresser of course.

"That's because I'm the first Mexican he's ever seen so he's got to compare me with Mexican's he knows." Jose went onto create a fictional scenario where Rose asked his drill sergeant if he was Michael Jordan. We all laughed and Rose responded tastefully by asking if when Jose had gotten out of the shower he'd dried his wet back. We would trade off insulting each other and laughing about it while drinking together the freedom in this was the creativity involved. Every time you pushed farther and harder to be offensive it was the job of the recipient to be even more jovial about receiving it. The greatest sign of weakness was to be frail enough to get touched by these jokes. I got called a Jewish banker and killed Jesus almost every night and with a smile each time. Rose was a Mormon with six mothers whose girlfriend wouldn't let his hand get higher then her left knee because God decreed Utah never to score. Jose generally got the illegal immigrant jokes and the Mexican jokes but he was ahead of any you could think of. He was from Texas.

Truly no three wiser men existed in Tongduchon, Korea ten miles from the DMZ as hallway light shown in on us and Jose yelled out into it for Private Vargas to have a drink with us. She was a little younger then Jose probably Rose's age and a thick girl with marvelous eyes that beamed, I think she was from New Mexico. She came in that night with her top plunging and her jeans constricting around her waist. She was in the same supply platoon Rose and Jose hailed from so she made a seat right in Jose's lap and helped herself to our liquor. The Crown Royal was really guest liquor so that no one dipped into our own good stash.

On this night Vargas didn't seem anything to us but a passing fancy just a fish in a great ocean and we had our own boat. I had been at Camp Nimble for half of a thousand years or eight months...maybe both by that time. Vargas called out to me as she left,

"Mr. White Folks, see you downtown." With a strange wink and twisting dance she was gone, out to begin the strange process of enticing people to buy her drinks and getting so savagely drunk that she could regret later the hedonistic joy of whatever she chose at that moment to do.

After she left we talked about her and how reasonably non-swanky she was but she was a Hispanic girl that Jose made clear went for the clean cut redneck types. The song Crossroads by Bone Thugs played and touched off a strange sentiment in Jose and I. We sang along closing our eyes and tightening the grip around our glass, it's a song about people dying and I remember the video because it had a computer generated Eazy-E ghost. Rose listened to rap in the casual way rock kids get into it where it's nice at the club and certainly a great excuse to grind on a girl you're afraid to tell you want affection from but not much more. He tapped at its flapping edges without ever finding its pulsating center so he thought our connection to this song was funny.

Suddenly Jose opened his eyes and let sentences form from him without the pre-fabrication of everyday speech. The words were like pins in a balloon. "My best friend man...fucking...got shot to death riding around Houston. We used to ride around all the time, take old ass cars and fix them up ourselves and just ride out you know. He got fucking shot just because he had a nice car, some retard thought he was fake cause he had money." As he finished his mouth curled at its edge. He tipped his cup just enough to spill the red Boone's Farm and SOJU mixture on the cheap blue carpeting under us. The same carpeting that was in everyone's room. I still recall how the liquor tumbled and spread out and how we all thought at once about nothing but that visual picture.

It must have been something even stranger for Rose. For the people that only know the flapping edges of a loosely constructed hip-hop culture pouring out a little liquor for your dead homie seems like the base ignorance of it all. It seems that way when you are far enough away or smart enough not to miss the dead. I am not.

Jose looked at me as he bobbed his head in rhythm with the song and I spoke "A friend of mine named Monkey overdosed not too long ago on heroin when he was in Thailand in the navy." I managed to say it authoritatively and match the authenticity of Jose's initial pouring onto the rug as I slowly changed my glasses position until the liquid was displaced on a spot not too far from Jose's. We talked about not being there for the funerals and birthdays and living without life. All the while we drank glass on top of glass chewing on the ice as it melted into smaller pieces.

Rose waited and nodded and sometimes participated but only when he felt some distance from our strange ritual did he ask the obvious question while pointing down at the deep stains on the rug "How are you going to get that out?"

I jumped in and answered "Utah, did you forget he's fucking his squad leader. He doesn't have to work that hard to pass room inspection." Laughing with a bellow felt good especially with the warm vibrating essence of all that liquor. Jose answered back right away. "No, you fuckers are making up shit I told you she was just helping me study." His squad leader was an odd Japanese woman from Oregon with naturally straight black hair who wanted Jose to become a Sergeant and was supposedly helping him study for the exam which was the first step.

"I've never seen anyone spend so much time studying." Rose turned to me and said in a falsely inquisitive tone. Jose would be the first dancing walrus before he would be a sergeant. We all knew that. "That's real dedication, huh." By now a gang of three, all Puerto Ricans from the fuel platoon, came in and asked us why the fuck we weren't downtown yet. I guess at that time we could think of no good reason so we went out with only three hours left until curfew knowing that the drinks downtown weren't like ours. The ice floated on a layer of water they tried to dilute the liquor with, not to keep us safe but to maintain their profit margin. Our liquor was pure and beautiful.

I remember never drinking before I met Jose's freezer. I drink now only to prove I could go back and conquer it.

Discerning Information

The sun is drowning the ground in light but somehow the warmth never makes it along with the illumination. If you looked out the window you would think the weather was amazing for this season, the type of day you need to take advantage of. Martin has his big tan coat zipped as high as it will go with the fur lined hood tight over his head. At the bus stop there are no misgivings about what kind of day it is; cold would be too kind a description. Martin worries his hot breath will come out of his mouth and freeze into a sculpture attached to his lips. He considers himself lucky when it doesn't.

His fingers tremble even in his thickest mittens. Not to say they don't make a difference but when the breeze picks up on a sub zero day like today nothing can help stop it. The bus had to be late on days like this when an extra ten minutes feels like the length of life multiplied by six and the only people outside don't have the ability to provide their own transit.

The important thing was to keep moving, don't stand in one place. In this weather a man who stands still enough can be frozen. Martin kept moving so his blood would do the same rubbing his mittens together and thinking hard enough to hope it fully heats his brain. The notice definitely wasn't going to be enough. It was too straight forward and Chomsky would never accept it alone. He spent all class trying to connect with all the kids through a series of references that were masterfully woven together to be topical enough to help him appeal to all the differing demographics in thc class.

Everyone liked him. Martin used to show up as early as he was capable having read over each word in the previous chapter so carefully he felt like he could teach it. Even to Chomsky.

A man had been walking or stumbling or a mixture of the two and all of a sudden stopped behind Martin. Scratching violently at his overgrown goatee the man leaned towards him. "This the bus stop?"

"Yeah man." That is what the big sign next to Martin saying bus stop has been trying to convey its whole life.

"Has it come yet?" The man didn't even seem cold. His sweater is light for this kind of weather.

"Nope."

The man has cheeks that wear a thousand nicks and scratches. He can't afford gloves so his hands are jammed in his pockets. If people are stars some shoot right into the ground like the sky wasn't meant for them. Martin meets so many of them of them riding the bus that he's numb too it. He remembers the man as a passenger without a destination. While most folks need a specific stop he just rides until one looks interesting enough to get off. It's only tragic the first time you ride with him and he talks to you the whole time even when you don't respond, every time after that it's just really annoying.

Martin stands on his tip toes and looks in both directions trying to make out a large form that might be over the horizon. His instincts are alert that the bus must be coming any second. It is just late enough for it to make perfect sense.

"Is that it?"

Martin squints and then turns to the man "Yeah Ralph it's coming."

So their knees knock together in anticipation of a heated place to sit and in reaction to a hard day in a tough season.

Every part of the bus whines as it comes to a stop. It seems like every part wants to be changed or lubricated or attended and hasn't been. The bus sounds so bad on days like this that if it stopped and literally fell to fragmented pieces Martin wouldn't be surprised. He would call a cab.

"Your name's Martin right?" This was always the setup question but he had no choice but to go for it.

"Yeah."

"Are you Mexican or what are you?" Most white people will ask the same question and it will take them three minutes to finish the request. They will spend all kinds of time being politically correct and blustering around it but Ralph didn't care. He also didn't remember.

"I'm Cuban." Martin's face holds solid as a rock partly due to the conversation and partly due to the lack of warmth in his environment.

"Oh…right…that was my second guess." For some reason Ralph would never forget Martin's name; it was locked in his head but his nationality was not. The first few times he tried to explain it but now he just tells him that he's Cuban, it ends the conversation quickly.

The door screams open and the bus driver is Martin's least favorite. He has gotten to know them all and the quirks that come along with them. This one has shaky hands and talks too much. He turns to Ralph who enters the bus first and stares him down hard from the end of his thick coke bottle glasses.

"You got the money, Ralph?"

He pats the driver on the shoulder twice and jams the dollar into the noisy device that takes them. "I've got it today. How are you Lester?"

"Oh you know, I'm happy to be in here and not out there." Martin walked up to the machine without saying anything and stuck his money in. Lester had continued to watch Martin more carefully then other passengers and Martin couldn't help but wonder if Lester was guessing what he was.

America is full of people who don't fit a singular ethnicity. For some reason people won't give up on trying to tag each person with their majority bloodline or discover any difference from their own. Martin wasn't more then thirty five percent Cuban but his features looked like he was more. To the world he allows himself to be Cuban because that's what they want. They want to know not out of idle curiosity; that's an overly simplistic view. It's the remains of a world that used to judge everyone by heritage (foolishly linking it to class) and misses it now that the times are changing.

After he takes his seat Martin pulls out a pad of paper he had hidden under his coat and a pen he had in his breast pocket. The form isn't good enough. Chomsky deserves more. He turns to the first blank page and writes in bolds CHOMSKY. As Martin started writing Ralph bore his eyes into the side of his head watching every movement of the young man's pen until Lester called out.

"Ralph, where you going today?"

He pulled his head away from Martin and looked up at the rearview mirror to see Lester's reflection. "No idea. Anywhere you'd recommend?"

"I don't know. Maybe you should go to the library. Warm place to read doesn't sound too bad."

They chatted back and forth loudly as Martin scratched and scrawled letters together to form thoughts. After he was done he re-read what he had to make sure it suited his intent. It read "I owe you an explanation so I'll give you this. I know you're trying to do something you think is noble by the way you teach. I know you think your reaching kids but I don't like it. You over simplify complicated things sometimes just so we'll pay attention. You make things so simple I know its not the truth."It was there that he stopped and tore the page out from the notebook wrinkled it up into a ball and stuffed it in his pocket. That was not going to work. It had to be declarative and give voice to his concerns, it couldn't hold back.

Ralph didn't even notice the turn of events as he was now staring into Lester's mirror having a conversation with his reflection.

Martin started again and this time wrote slower but started the same way with CHOMSKY in bold letters but the rest was different. This time he read it to himself as he wrote it "How could you teach kids that Karl Marx never failed? How could you tell them that what he said was meaningful? Why is he in every class I attend? He was somehow a philosopher, economist, and sociologist. I think all the teachers just like him because he's the Madonna of political theory- he won't say anything important but he stays dropping controversial remarks. That's why I hate your class. You try so hard to make kids listen that you forget your teaching garbage sometimes. I might not even go to school anymore, I might just work and study on my own. I don't know if I can learn inside a system like this where everyone sells their opinion like its fact to kids too young to know the difference. Just because a bunch of people agree on something doesn't make it a fact; that just makes it popular. I don't know what I'm going to do but I'm going to start by dropping your class. I've appreciated your time and you've taught me a lot about not being in so much of a rush to learn that you forget to second guess the messenger."

He signed it and jammed the drop slip in between the letter and the next page. He put the notebook down next to him and Ralph didn't waste any time.

"What were you writing Martin?"

"Leave the boy alone Ralph!" Lester looked up at Ralph in his rear view mirror.

Martin smirked. Lester thought he was going to get up and throttle the strange homeless man because he had some sort of intense ethnic temper that couldn't be cooled. "I was just writing a letter to one of my teachers." He said it in a particularly calm way to sway Lester away from his assumptions.

Ralphs eyebrows got worried, the hairs stood on end. "Is he a bad teacher?"

He kicked his feet up on the back of the seat in front of him and considered the prospect. Chomsky had worked so hard for so long to be so good, Martin could tell. He had to be honest. "I don't think he's bad he's just no good for me."

Ralph nodded a lot and Lester didn't say anything. The next stop came and a group of fourteen year old girls all walked in together. They were in the middle of an exciting conversation that meant nothing at all but was carried on with a lot of energy. It broke the communication between Lester, Ralph and Martin for the remainder of the trip until Martin got off at the university and Lester turned to him as he left.

"You have a good day, son. Good luck."

Martin thanked him and didn't smile but he was about to let one slip and Lester could see it and smiled for him as he pulled the lever that opened the door.

Dippin' Dots are NOT the Future

The Pineview Mall has eighty five stores crammed into it most of which are unnecessary copies of the original forty six. Back in the mid eighties it only had one place for pretzels The Precious Pretzel but things have changed. Now there are four or five places some just offering pretzels and lemonade some offering hot dogs and ice cream as well. Benny and Peter have been walking the mall since the early nineties, they spent hours and probably years of their life in the food court waiting for slices of over priced pizza to be served up to them. They never assumed they would grow out of it and as man children they wouldn't want to. The mall is all they know.

Benny is a small man diminutive in height weight and tone, when he speaks his words are light and listless as if they don't mind if they go unheard. The only one that listens to him is his mother and Pete who stands in contrast. He speaks wild and carelessly as if his thoughts validate themselves through birth. Pete is a husky man not all that much taller than Benny but someone who can't be ignored, a fat man who dances with his shoulders when he talks. Benny blinks three times and then stutters into the end of a thought.

"I...You would feel different about video games if you played the right ones. You should check out The Devil May Cry series." He looks up at Pete as he finishes.

"I told you I can't do the whole video game thing, I work long hours man with a lot of shit I have to take care of. Why should I come home after a long day of being told by my boss that I keep messing stuff up and then play for the fate of the universe or the love of the princess or to avenge my wife and kids...then mess that up too. It's just too much defeat in one day. The video games I was into were about as complex as fitting the right shaped block in the right space."

Benny shrugs his shoulders letting the subject go, the more you pursue a debate with Pete the more he chews it over, lunging forward having to win it. For a minute or two it is quiet between them as they walk slowly taking in the home goods stores and the athletic gear outlets. They watch an old couple on the bench yell at each other and a young couple lovingly grab each others anal passage. Benny begins to take in the sounds. First he hears people chewing and slurping then the deafening echo of a hard, loud mumble. It is a song playing from the mall's muzak system which seems to be a heavy duty blues song performed passionately by Charlie Brown's Teacher.

"Who is this? What is he saying?" Benny's eyebrows wrinkle in confusion having rarely heard such a strange tune in the mall. The song has piano in it and a flute he thinks.

"This is Van Morrison, man. The song is....uhh...Moondance it's the one in all the pub jukebox's."

"What is he talking about?"

"Fucking. All Van Morrison songs are in some way about fucking. He's actually the best white musician to ever sing about fucking. Mumbling is just his thing it's the whole coded language of the hippie. It must be pretty cool to make music that a whole generation fucked to, I mean that's a helluva feeling."

"I don't know..." Benny scratches the outer edge of his nose trying to somehow convince the mucus inside to stay content if it won't leave. "...sounds gross."

"Benny! Don't act like your some kind of wet noodle, I've seen you in action. You're an animal!" Pete's shoulders begin to do the Oompa Loompa dance as he raises his tone to a volume that interests the high school kids in a big lumpy group behind them. "Remember when that stripper stuck that piece of licorice in her...womb you ATE THAT SHIT!!! HA!" The kids rattle from side to side processing the loud nasty proclamation. Benny is no stranger to being humiliated by the hefty showman and he went back and forth on how deliberate it all was.

"I don't remember that."

Pete smirks and shrugs letting the topic go and giving into the comfortable silence, most of the time Benny liked the silence better then the conversation. It's possible that the stark contrast between the two caused his affection for the quiet that was the Tao of Benny.

Steve had on baggy cargo shorts, the style that you buy looking ragged and faded already with a red and white polo shirt, the collar flipped up of course. Steve is a key guy to be friends with. For some reason Steve is so marvelously generic that everyone loves him. Every important party is at Steve's three bedroom townhouse. He's more popular then sugar free gum. Part of Pete's never ending philanthropy is that he schmoozes with Steve so Benny doesn't have to; Benny can just walk with Pete and he's in. Steve is not alone. A few yards behind him, sipping delicately at a small coke, is his current girlfriend, Missy.

"Steve, how is the end of summer treating you? Is it a time for reflection or simply a new chapter in the luminous volume of you?" Steve doesn't understand what any of that was but he throws a wiry arm over Pete's shoulder and chirps quick jerky chunks of thought.

"Pete...I got to talk to you man" Steve swings his head back and yells over to Missy. "I got to talk to my bro real quick. I'll be right back, babe." He maintains his arm lock around Pete and pulls him along beside him while Benny like Tonto trails behind the two.

"Pete, this girl is WILD. I'm telling you I've never been in a situation like this man. She is crazy!"

"That's great to hear; isn't she kinda weird? Doesn't talk much and when she drinks too much she cries for no damn reason. Is any of that going on?" Whenever Pete wants to broach a subject with care and can't figure out how to he disregards the care and just broaches the shit out of it. He is physically unhappy with being held in this manner by Steve. Both Benny and Pete treasure their personal space and don't like any kind of man hug-snuggle situation. Pete now waits as Steve thinks over the questions he raised.

"Sure she's into all that but she is a champ in the bedroom; I mean really knows what's going on. Sometimes I like a little music going while I'm doing it, you know, like when you work out at the gym. Anyway, I was looking through her CD's and wanted to put on some groovy stuff, you know, so I can keep my rhythm. I put on the Curtis Mayfield and she takes it to a whole different place! When Curtis Mayfield puts it down she takes control buddy and will do anything...I mean...anything."Pete shakes his head puckering his lips and letting out a low whistle a response of pure admiration.

"So you're listening to less Fall Out Boy these days." Steve gives an emphatic nod then continues as the group walks right past the weave store.

"Bro I'm on E-bay trying to find import live albums, unreleased tracks you don't even know. This girl is draining me and it's pretty fucking cool. Too bad that dude died man, the selection is limited you know."

Pete pushes out his bottom lip and asks "Did you try other stuff like James Brown or Stevie Wonder...?"

Steve waves his hand and closes his eyes briefly for effect before re-opening them "I'm telling you it's got to be Curtis Mayfield or nothing at all. I mean if you played The Superfly soundtrack she'd blow me in front of my parents."

"That's love." The words are soft and lazy. They are Benny's and come from behind the two men. Pete smiles gratified that Benny likes to shit on people too. The arm that has kept Pete in place next to Steve falls suddenly as he looks back and forth between both men.

"Yeah it is, but anyway I got to talk later she's probably waiting for me." He smiles at the end signifying that even though he hasn't figured out the best way to take full long term advantage of this situation he is greatly enjoying it. Steve walks away sweating, wondering maybe it is weird that she cries when she drinks. He ambles off leaving only the sound his flip flop's make against the floor.

This topic is easily discussed with no argument between Benny and Pete for a good half hour and in conclusion they like the situation. If indeed the girl is crazy she can be helped and become less crazy but great sex...life changing super sex is not a regular occurrence. No point in a good sane nice lady dating Steve anyway.

As they plod along they stumble upon a well developed kiosk labeled Dippin'Dots, the whole stand is light blue such a light blue it is very unseemly. A color that deviates so greatly from the real color blue it is somehow against nature, in opposition to blue. The island of merchandising is not nearly as ugly as the hat that lays limply on the ruffled black hair of the attendant who manages it.

The attendant makes eye contact with the two men knowing by the way they stand in shock that they have no experience or understanding of Dippin' Dots. He begins a pre-formulated sales pitch, "Hello my name is Brian and I'm here to introduce you to the next level of taste and goodness beyond what you used to know as ice cream.

We start with the finest dairy ingredients, then add taste-tempting flavorings and special "goodies" to produce all our delicious flavors and flavor combinations. Dippin' Dots are then flash-frozen using a special cryogenic process. This super-cold freezing allows our products to maintain their individual "dot" consistency. Dippin' Dots are then transported coast-to-coast and around the world by truck, train, plane and ship. Our saying is true when you think about it Dippin' Dots are the ice cream of the future." Brian smiles weakly as if someone pressed a button on his back that's labeled smile.

Brian speaks directly to Pete trying to pitch as directly and naturally as he can which gives Benny time to look the station over. Beyond the obscene color he notices one other thing and addresses Pete about it immediately "Hey, did you see this..." He points down at a short sentence on the side of the station just under the Technicolor logo; Pete turns in a cagey fluid motion and reads the sentence. It reads Dippin' Dots Ice Cream of The Future but after Future is a capital R with a circle around it which signifies the corporate bodies registered trade marking of it. Pete is thrown and his neck jerks back bringing his vision back to Brian who he now feels is a guilty party or at least the representative for one.

"Brian!! Dippin' Dots are the future?" His head cocks to the side like a movie dinosaur.

"Well, it's really the technology and development of ice cream you know..." Brian is smirking and vocally prancing when Pete lunges forward and slams his fist on the counter top in front of him, everything halts temporarily.

"Brian do you know what this trademark means? In a literal sense it means that Dippin' Dots owns the future. If I want to write a screenplay where I fuck your mother and name it Pete is the future they can sue me. GOD DAMMIT BRIAN we can't let these fat cat pricks buy our future and brand it their own. It's fucking people that built these walls that built this nation not loosely knit groups of elitist businessman. I know what you're thinking." Brian is stiff as celery just waiting for the insane man to stop. " You're going to tell me that the existence of these multi-national corporate entities gave me my mp3 player and my multi-colored shoe laces. You know what my answer to that is? What happens when it breaks down? What happens your precious economic system dies the same awful death every other one has? At that point it's me and it's you...sharp sticks and wild animals. We're the fucking future."

When Brian began his pitch he was drifting through the words. He had said them so much so many times that they were friends of his that sounded nice. He loved saying that it was a Cryogenic process and the way people looked at him all excited like he really sold futuristic Blade Runner ice cream but now he is shaken as if physically accosted. He sweats greasy beads of glimmering sweat and the mall lights shine on him like interrogation lights, licking his lips and trying to wet his dry dead mouth. He listens as the man opposed to him identifies his terror and jumps back on him.

"I will leave you alone after you do something for me. I want you to say...NO FUCK THAT...I want you to yell it out. I want you to open your arms and yell 'BRIAN IS THE FUTURE'. So that when it's me, you and the wild boars I'll know your down to use a sharp stick." Brian starts to speak he even raises his left hand using his pointer finger to ask lightly with his body language if he can debate the topic. Pete again slams his fist into the demonic blue counter that separate's them. Ripples of fear tremble through Brian and before he can think over the philosophical debate he bellows.

"BRIAN IS THE FUTURE! I AM THE FUTURE!!!" Benny shakes his head pretending that he doesn't enjoy the display acting like he believes the man has been somehow humiliated. After a moments perspective dons on him he realizes that this is false; that the man has been humiliated by that awful hat and that awful act he has to put on.

He agrees with what Pete would say which is that the bending and pulling at Brian will only tighten him up until he gets to snap back and when Brian snaps back the world will change. Eventually.

The Wise Man and the One Who Talks

It's not a tiny bar by any means but certainly not built big enough to house the people who love Gordon Pope. I can name at least five people off the top of my head who were in that crowd and would kill for Gordon Pope. It's not all that difficult because I'm one of them and I'm a pacifist.

I used to drink nights like this down greedily. Loving the company of so many different people and the city on any day of the week would open its mouth for me and gargle excitement loud enough to be heard in the boonies. That was before I moved to the boonies.

People were mashed in shoulder to shoulder laughing uncomfortably and waiting for a glimmer of his attention, except for the seated inner group. As I walked in I got a good look at him before his eyes made it over to me. He was sitting there with an open green beer turning his head thoughtfully, slowly and smiling at each member of the seated group. Somehow he made each smile different for them and personal to them. If you have a thousand friends or ten thousand you still probably only have six of them who you count as upper tier; the people who would never fuck you out of anything not for fear of retribution but because they love you.

When he finally senses me looking at him, his gaze turns on the crowd and he picks me out instantly. His eyes open wide and his mouth doesn't smile, it jumps aghast and calls.

"Dave!" He motions me over with a hand tough enough to beat the tops off bottles but soft enough to powder baby butt cheeks. He uses those hands to signal that space must be made. He uses those hands to serve a lot of these people every night and listen to them. Some of them only know him as calm and mature not like he used to be. I was walking over to see him and go back to standing in the crowd but by the time I'm in his presence a seat has been cleared. "Sit down."

It is too bad for me that the seat was next to the biggest ugliest prick on my top ten list of biggest ugliest pricks. Popo has a name that is much too long and much too Italian for anyone he knows to say properly so there was a natural shortening that came quite easily. You can't be that interested in the actual name and if you are its really too bad I have no idea how its spelled or pronounced. I hate trying for twenty minutes for the right way to say it only to have a hundred people scoff at me. It will remain a mystery to you. He's not dumb but he does look like a goon, an awkwardly sized person without the intimidating aura to make it make sense.

He was always the type to make scathingly aggressive jokes to you but to become easily overly sensitive at a response. That was before but I don't forget.

"How you doing man? Haven't seen you in a while." I do my best to push out an overworked smile as I speak. The remark is always a stupid thing to say because we both know there is a reason we don't see each other. He turns to me flapping his big Joe Camel sized face and smiles.

"Yeah. I been good." He faded back and let the shadows eat him out of my sight. I turned to Gordon.

"So your turning thirty…got a kid now and married! Who ever thought you'd get here from where you were?"

He didn't verbally respond but he shook his head to acknowledge the shared amazement.

His wife was relaxed and happy next to him holding onto his arm, she spoke. "Pretty soon it will be your turn."

I shrugged. I hate when guys get all freaked out in response to this kind of joking. They spin their heads and look shocked as if to say "WITH THAT LADY? NO WAY!" Which is not entirely complimentary. I shrug because if it happens it happens; I have plans for it when it does, I have plans if it doesn't, we'll see.

"How's Emily?"

Gordon's wife and I both have a powerful ability to direct oratory exchange and maintain it far past the need for the conversation. We are talkers and there is some weird combination of being raised in a chatty household and being born with it that makes us able to talk with force and energy until no one wants to involve themselves they just want to watch. I begin by talking about Emily and that leads to comparative stories about things couples do. She fit wonderfully into his life the way Emily does in mine. She had her own large group of friends she had always successfully maneuvered so his was not strange or daunting.

"Where is Emily?" I told her that my fiancé was sick and maybe she was. Sick of tight spaces and loud noise, sick of always having to meet up with various groups of my friends but she had no idea it was his birthday. I didn't either until I got here. Gordon texted me minutes ago just saying it would mean a lot if you could come by. I don't remember the dates of anyone's birthday, its not only his that slips my mind. My friends all take turns forgetting each others and then kicking ourselves but never hard enough to remember next year.

People are huddled right behind the inner circle throwing in little funny bits of conversation and Gordon fields each one with his complete attention. It feels like a celebrity giving really genuine time to speak with his fans as he signs autograph after autograph to his grateful public. He doesn't think of it that way. He likes all of them and listens that's it. I'm the one over thinking things.

Popo was never this quiet before. It is always awkward when people disappear like he did. I remember him kicking me out of the bar because the Yankees beat the Red Sox and I was smiling like I fed dirt to his cat. We just weren't ever meant to be in the same room for that long, I'm not even sure I understand it.

When he disappeared I was happy and I didn't keep it a secret. Gordon never judged me for it as I tore his ex-roommate down and outright implied that he got what was coming to him. He just told me that he still speaks to him regularly and eventually he had a new job and was doing well at it. He was so civil I mirrored it and eventually stowed away the residual bad blood acknowledging the progress.

Now he was right next to me and calling out to Gordon casually. "Hey, I got you a present." His giant calloused paws reached over and beyond me handing a package in white wrapping to Gordon. The gift was quite obvious due to the nature of its shape but even more obviously odd as a result.

I stood up and walked to the bar. I needed a drink and now. The moisture had jumped ship from my mouth and all of a sudden when my tongue moved I could hear a dry wrinkling sound. It was as if the moisture gave its resignation from my insane stupidity.

Popo had amazing control. The bartender turned and looked right at me while I was shaking my head, staring at the big noble goof.

"Can I help you sir?"

I whipped my head to him "White Russian, please."

I hate being wrong. I just can't stand it. I can remember all the things I've done wrong in list form and rank them, all the false information that I stood on because I'm more bull headed then determined to be right and I'm very determined to be right.

Gordon opens it and acts surprised but he's not. Its Jamison whiskey and he loves it. He's stocking a healthy liquor cabinet at his new house because he loves alcohol and grown ups get to have a liquor cabinet. You're wondering why it's a weird gift, one that makes me understand how much of a dirty bag of poo I am. I'll explain.

Gordon and I were perfect roommates. I loved to stay at home and watch old movies and boxing while he loved to go out and socialize and so he dragged me out of the apartment when I felt more of a connection with Rita Hayworth then any living woman. I kept him inside when days out in a row sapped his natural strength and he didn't want to have to say no. He got a great job at the best bar in this fake big city and Popo loved him immediately.

Popo had worked there for years so when he loved someone everyone else at the bar did too but his personality was overbearing and he had issues with control. Long story short: Popo was the saddest drunk who ever lived. Most people who I've known who were alcoholics drank not only to have, but to be, fun. It no longer gave them the fluid joy and relaxation in the moment like it had in the past and they wanted to think it could do that again. They believed in the power it used to have. Popo was never like that.

Today he sits smiling and laughing gently as he bobs his head and his hands don't shake at all. All those nights when he took Gordon out and got disgusting end-of-days-last-call-drunk and the next morning when he would wake up and keep it going all the way till he got to work. He would take little hits of whatever his flavor of the day was at work until they had an intervention that didn't get the point across. A call to arms he blew off.

The people that are standing now stand a little quieter. They have the respect not to whisper. So many people came here because he loves people enough to never doubt them. When Popo went to rehab after a torturous stretch where he was let go by the bar, Gordon never ceased contact. He would wear Popo's achievements on his face and say "I'm proud of that dude" and I would nod.

So many people disappear and come back with six pack in hand claiming not to be alcoholics; they will swear that to you. Popo purchased that bottle, the same one that used to drink him night into day and then back into the evening, he controlled it and gave it away. He held it and shuffled it off. Gordon took it as a simple gift, a drink he would enjoy. It didn't symbolize any great internal strength, Gordon knew all along about his friends' strengths. Hence the faith.

The crowd didn't though. The crowd was full of old drinking buddies that were there for the good times and the end. When they saw him pull an object up and it was a bottle in his hand they had to have lost breath for a second before regaining it. I couldn't face him. Son of a bitch had abandoned his whole personality of being a son of a bitch. How much of the person I hated wasn't a person, but a liquid living in him and gutting his positive traits? I hate being wrong.

The White Russian was awful but I tipped him anyway.

Popo kept my seat for me and when I plopped down next to him a funny thing happened. We started laughing. He wasn't that different, still a guy who poked at you to make himself laugh but there was careful consideration in his words now. He held himself upright and spoke when he needed too, not to validate that he was there. He had the confidence of a man who had just come from hell and was having a great time now that he left.

He kept by Gordon's side all night buying him drinks and the story goes that later on as he got more and more drunk Popo helped him maintain and then they stopped. At a decent hour everyone went home, Gordon to his wife and his baby and Popo to his apartment and his television.

I guess I went home and grumbled like Elmer Fudd.

I was no longer mad at Popo and haven't caught myself being mad at him since. This is an achievement because I tend to maintain hard feelings long after they are useful. I am now a little mad at Gordon, or maybe jealous, for being so right so damn much.

Friends Like These

The cold is different in a tent. We have a thick black summer sleeping bag that we get into at night and once were in it we pull the colossal green winter sleeping bag over that one. The cold is not an annoyance but a dreadful reality. Cocooned in both sleeping bags and wrapped in a camouflage green blanket we sleep on cots trying to keep the sensitive parts of our body away from the metal framework of it.

Outside I have been told its zero degrees and when they wake me up in the morning I'm confident I will grasp it even more. The worst is how cold your boots are after being underneath your cot all night, just freezing and hardening. The days in the field are usually pretty miserable, just for the sheer length of the day. By the time you setup a perimeter and figure out a guard roster you're pooped and then some. So the highlight of the day is the night and its fragile precious silence. I always sleep with hands on my nuts. It's hard to elaborate on this statement in a way that makes it sensible but suffice it to say that its good to know you still have them at the end of every day.

All lined up in two rows inside the tent we have no heating system other then these wonderful sleeping bags we all have pulled well over our heads. I have one last vital conversation to have before I sleep.

"Singleton?!"

"What is it Davis."

"What if you were promoted..."

"Never happen." She cuts me off but I continue.

"...but you get promoted to Sergeant in charge of cleanliness. You have to inspect us all and make sure we don't smell like ass."

Her voice comes slowly "What...the fuck are you talking about?"

"You line us all up in formation and have to smell our armpits, all that stuff. Who do you think would stink the worst?"

I see Singleton so much I can see her just by listening to her talk. I can see that mouse nose she has and the brown eyes. The military uniform doesn't do much for the female figure but she looks good to all of us. Could stand to be a little bit taller, maybe. The boom box has long been turned off and the card games folded a half hour ago. All the side conversations had just started to falter. Everybody long back from the showers they listen in on my scenario now wondering what her response will be.

"Jamaica."

Jamaica is directly parallel to our conversation wrapped in a cot shivering angrily. Everyone laughs because they know that he leaves his crap everywhere and they can picture his face wrinkling in anger inside the sleeping bag. Nobody really feels any particular way about Jamaica other then Michaels who beat him like a dirty rug.

Good thing too because if I heard Jamaica launch into his storied history as an undercover cop again I think I would snap. Jamaica lies not to improve his image, you can tell by the energy he uses doing it that he just views it as a part of what conversation is. Like when the Apache's used to shoot a wounded animal take that sucker home and tell everyone they had a glorious showdown with him. The art of bullshiting. Michaels is different. He's a simple guy, black kid from Philadelphia damn near amateur level boxer but you'd think he was kind of stupid if he wasn't good natured enough to make you forget. Michaels got sick of it and told him to shut up, Jamaica grabbed and lifted him off his feet but didn't pin his arms back. Poor Jamaica.

"Why, Jamaica?" I ask it, happy that my name wasn't her answer.

"I'm just saying...all the crap he leaves everywhere. Yesterday he was laying with his feet out and OH MY GOD. I thought I was going to die!"

At this point Jamaica's dark face leaps out from the night his eyes half closed in a mean squint He yells out "Bombaclot!" which he might as well trademark. The women who've dissatisfied him have all fallen into this broad group only one got angry turning to him in formation and letting him know she knew what it meant. I had to google it and I guess it means "Cunt" but originally it was a cloth women used as a tampon. I'll tell you that cloth is probably WAY more useful then Jamaica when it's time to get work done.

The word's cartoonish emphasis gets the same reaction a Tim Allen grunt elicits. The crowd goes wild. I'll bet Tim Allen has said the C word more then I have. Just a feeling I guess.

Singleton doesn't do anything crazy or get offended. Singleton is the winner. In real life Jamaica got engaged to an attractive woman back home and then came back here to base and immediately started cheating on her. His plan was that he could cheat it all out of his system and then be domestic. He told us all about it and was very proud but she dumped him before the wedding. Singleton is a study in the other direction.

She is married and pretends domesticity until Mr. Singleton (who is a nut by the way) goes out to the field for training. She has a band of guys that go over her house and smoke a little, and sleep over. No one calls her out for it, no one tells her husband. You don't tell on your friends, your squad, your people. But I would never fuck with her. I couldn't help but think of that skinny weirdo somewhere in his tent inside two sleeping bags thinking about life with his wife and the future. Sucker hitched himself to the wrong star and even if he gets a picket fence it ain't going to be white.

The laughter dies a pleasant death in the frigid air. I can hear from her breathing that she's fallen asleep. She doesn't snore but sounds kind of like a dog, nothing but heavy breaths. You got to be careful sleeping in the field. These fucks love to play jokes on you in the middle of the night put whip cream all over your mouth and act like they just made sweet monkey love to your unconscious body or duct tape you to the cot using so much of the stuff your arms hurt. I've never been taken but that doesn't mean anything. It only takes once with friends like these.

The Purple Finch

I never thought having a pet would be this completely wretched. It's possible that my choice of pets is at fault and that if I had chosen a fat lazy cat to love me in a purely passive way it would be much better. For some reason I had to have a bird and I found one, a gorgeous purple finch that I named Martin. He had such nobility when we first met he would stand all day with his beak in the air. It sounds very strange but he reminded me of my grandfather. He would nod to me on a good day and flutter closer acknowledging me in that quiet loving way, and on a bad day would look away as if he expected so much more from me.

All of that is gone a honeymoon stage I can barely remember. Today I look into Martin's cage and he just howls in that annoying chirpy voice, never stopping for a breath. He torments me in the most abusive manipulative way. If you remember that old saying "a little bird told me," he's telling me all right blathering his terrible bird speak until the migraine returns to me. The migraine that's as familiar to me as my own hand, it pulsates and stabs at the inside of my pudgy skull. It's that damn bird! I will not take his insults anymore!

"Listen to me Martin if you do not stop this horrible noise I will grab your universe by the bars pick it up and throw you out of my window!" As I complete my insulting digression I shake his cage and rattle it as viciously as I can. Martin doesn't change his expression he just flutters in place watching me go out of my mind.

I stop my attack on the cage only when my energy dwindles leaving me the dreadful want to…kill that bird so I can go to sleep. I sleep every night but its not good sleep sometimes I wonder if I should even try sleeping in my current situation. If I do get to sleep like man is intended, that luscious peaceful sleep owed to paupers and princes it will be because that bird let me sleep and has loosened his tyrannical grip on my existence… or because I threw him out of my fourth story window.

The naked eye observer would consider Martin a beautiful bird, a purple finch is a wonderful sight, Martin's head is a mild purple bordering on bright red. The color runs down his neck where it mix's with the lighter feathers on his breast plate. Bird watchers and environmentalists wet themselves taking in Marin's appearance all the while unaware that he has a dirty malignant character. I take full responsibility for being fooled, the same way a cruel unfeeling woman can be wrapped in a tempting guise of natural beauty.

I need to get out of the living room Martin dominates so I stand up and walk away from him trying to find the refrigerator. I cross into the kitchen where the birds cries were farther away, less potent. I have half a gallon of orange juice left so I grab a pint glass and fill it half way. After the orange juice is back in its rightful place I open the freezer and drop some ice cubes into the beverage. This is my favorite drink the most acidic potent and unforgiving of any natural beverage. Truthfully apple juice is orange juice's little sister and prune juice and grapefruit juice are for psychopaths. I can think of nothing more repulsive then…

"Leo!" My back is to the sound but who could be speaking? My door is locked and no one is here but me and…"Leo I know your having problems we should talk about it."

My hand shakes like a leaf knocking the ice cubes from one side of the glass to the other I respond in a rushed worried way that doesn't serve me well "Martin, is this some kind of joke?"

"Joke! Why don't we talk about you LOSING YOUR JOB last week that was funny right?" He pulled his beak up in the air challenging me to answer him.

"You're a bird you don't even have a job how could you know how hard it is keeping a career on track." For some reason I calm down and decide that if Martin and I must carry on in this way it should be a proper sharing of ideas.

"You don't think this is a job! You're my job you damn dope! Your constant depressing loneliness will drive us both out of house and home if someone doesn't take charge." He swings his tiny head from side to side his feathers ruffling he opens up his wings, gloating.

"And you think you're the one who should take charge." My voice drones and dies I can't help but think maybe I'm nuts.

"I just want to work with you for us to make a REAL difference for both of us…" I look away from him down at the dirty dark blue rug that's been under my feet for years as he continues "…Leo…are you with me on this!"

"Whatever is best Martin. Whatever is right."

A cloud of angry smoke is blown right between Steve and Ben. Walter did it intentionally, daring the smug duo to speak up. Steve pulls the lever on the side of the easy chair, making it easier to recline away from the hostile gas. Ben leans forward staring at Walter who appears to be on the brink of lashing out at the world.

"Another game?" Walter breaths deeply through his nose and uses it to flex his near six foot two hundred pound physique. He jabs a finger towards the television behind him where a cheerleader appears mid-jump a look of victorious euphoria mocking Steve and Ben.

"Fuck that." Ben hurls the two words at his nemesis while Walter smiles. Through the smoke his smile is the only thing visible aside from his bright red hair.

"You guys are pussies that's all!" His smile widens and the hair on his arms becomes erect staring the two down. In the background Renee shakes her head and sips gently out of an oddly formed tall glass of apple juice. She's emaciated in an almost attractive way and her voice, when she speaks, is gruff and deep. Steve only glances at her while remaining fully reclined; he's forming thought weaponry to hurl at Walter.

"Every time we play Madden you get crazy. If you win you talk about it for twenty minutes and if you lose you start fights." Ben looks over, surprised by Steve's willingness to confront Walter after years of his scary unpredictable actions.

Walter's shock manifested itself in terrible glee, his words sounded like boulders. "Both of you ladies know the truth that's why you want out. You know that even if we play sixty more games tonight I will beat you every time. I'll drink and drink all the while beating the snot out of you homos!"

Ben gets more comfortable laying back into the couch having dominance over something. "You're the man, huh? What makes you soooo much better than everyone?"

"I never fucking said that I'm unbeatable at Madden or the toughest mother fucker in the world. There's probably somebody in Thailand right now who would beat my ass at this game! I do however maintain that none of you sorry pricks stand a chance in hell when my hand grips that controller. I'm like Picasso with a blank canvas or Al Pacino playing a Hispanic gangster. If you refuse to continue I will consider it a complete submission to my superior abilities." It's important to note that as Walter speaks his face contorts like a parent's or a school teacher's does when commanding children.

"How did you get this stupid Walter? Even if you are better at this stupid game than anyone in the universe your still twenty-eight and living at your mom's house."

Renee simply can't take it anymore; a pouch of cocaine in her back pocket is burning a hole in it, like money does to someone at a casino. Ben told her that after this game was over they would all go into the bathroom and indulge. She can live without it but why should she have to for this dialogue?

Steve and Ben look at each other understanding how bad this could get. Walter enjoys creating conflict and doesn't take well to jabs at his ego. Walter begins pacing from the television towards the kitchen and then back seemingly deep in drunken thought. His speech seems to come as his thoughts do, completely unfiltered. "So you're telling me that I'm a failure, even if I am the supreme Madden player and can drink any of you women under the table? Are you a success?" He jabs inquisitively at Renee in a way that confounds her angry haze.

"Fuck you Walter!"

"Exactly! Fuck me I'm a failure but what about your boy Ben? Is he a failure like me? If not why is he here…in this room…LOSING to me?" As the sentence dramatically closes the maniacal pirate comes closer and closer to Renee.

"Walter, chill the fuck out." Ben refuses to leave his seat and be concerned after all how bad could it get? Steve is not holding up as well, being a mild associate of the group he's never seen Walter's stunts before. His brow has been gathering sweat at a steady disconcerting rate and even though he wouldn't dream of jumping into the conversation at this point. If he did his cries would be bloody desperation.

Walter turns for a moment observing Ben's patient masked amusement then snaps back around heading towards Renee slowly, methodically, and with complete confidence. He pulls a cream colored Bic lighter from the depths of his left pocket. Snapping at its trigger a few times sparks begin emerging from it as he re-enters the argument he created.

"I know you might find this hard to believe but I love all of you! Not the kind of love Renee's into where I'm going to fuck you and then take your rent money more like a football coach. I simply want Steve and Ben to be the best that they can be and to insure they grow and improve," Walter holds his right hand straight out so his fingers almost touch Renee's nose. Renee's eyes squint and tighten in a cutting hurtful way, but before anyone notices Walter brings the lighter in his left hand under his right. The flame slaps and grabs at his palm while he continues his diatribe. “To insure that the big bad failure gets to play just one more fucking game with the two little failures before they run off, do coke, and try and get you excited enough to do things your known around the state for…I will do anything.” Her anger starts to subside as the smell of burning flesh overcomes her and she goes from the first stage of dealing with Walter to shock. Not only the smell but the illumination has made the inside of his hand so much more visible to her in the most terrible way.

She cries in the most anti-climactic way. Finally not having capability to fight back the tears. Submission as Walter would call it the streams of light water rush out of her face just missing the glass of apple juice that rattles and shakes in her weakened grip. His laugh marks the end of the stunt; he tosses the lighter onto the kitchen counter behind her.

He spins around smiling from ear to ear making a physical motion similar to the one Fonzie made on Happy Days when things had gone just as planned. Ben shook his head and picked up the jet-black console attached to the Playstation two, while Steve uncorked a fresh beer sucking urgently from it. As Walter stepped over Steve and regained his controller all he could think of was which team he hadn’t won with yet. Renee went to the bathroom alone.

From the bathroom window a fire is visible and if Renee cared she would take a moment to observe the four people sitting around it. They all have a Pabst Blue Ribbon either in hand or seated nearby and an open twelve pack sits next to Charles on the extreme right of their formation. Charles is wearing a black dress shirt with a huge collar that exposes his forty two year old chest hair; he fidgets incessantly in silence waiting for Emily to get off the phone. Her left hand flails dramatically while she emphatically describes Charles unfeeling nature to her best friend Joanne. Audrey doesn’t pay attention to Emily in general but especially tonight, tonight she’s drifting in thought staring distantly into the fire. She’s thinking about Gordon, which is funny only because Gordon is thinking about her.

Gordon is trying to find any pattern or reasoning behind the random instances of romantic interest Audrey has shown throughout the year and a half they’ve shared as “friends.” He’s drifting off too in a way thinking about the first time they drank together at a party she threw. Her Auburn hair was long and perfect like it is today and her body lithe and muscular; she’s even more bubbly and energetic. Even when she was her most inebriated they could talk and just laugh. That night

Gordon made up in his mind he didn't want to be her friend, but he would if he failed to mate with her. Every few months she would get real drunk, throw her arms around him and talk, talk about how men suck and how he was the only person she could count on. She would passionately embrace him and they would kiss sometimes over and over for hours and other times one big drunk kiss would come just before she got too drunk to function. He always tucked her in and let her sleep it off. The next day was the problem; it just didn't remember the night before.

Once he drifts back, he notices Audrey has shifted her field of vision and cocked her head staring at him. She's wearing all white pants and shirt with a lightweight tan jacket a size too large for her. Her legs extended out in a fluid sultry way and she spoke first. "Penny for your thoughts."

"I was wondering how Walter's doing he's been drinking all day."

"Walter's an asshole."

"I know." A slim cool grin jogged across Gordon's face as Charles decided to jump in the conversation until Emily got off the phone.

"He's a prick. If he wasn't friends with Ben nobody would hang out with that fuck."

All in a matter of seconds Emily slams her flip phone shut and Charles swivels with open arms of confusion forming words with his mouth that never come out. By the time his mouth opens she's already stood up, dusted herself off and started a fast scamper to the house. Emily has a thicker fuller body than Audrey not in any adverse way it just makes her exit more dramatic Gordon and Charles notice her bounce and jiggle on her way out. Charles doesn't have time to excuse himself especially with Emily's history of extreme depression; he just bolts, whispering her name angrily.

Gordon and Audrey notice and find each other's gaze again. Gordon identifies her glossy stare and quickly curtails the moment with a question. "How's your boyfriend doing?"

"Jim? I don't know. He still hasn't found a job." The effect is immediate and her shoulders slouch. Her eyes drift again but not in a far off romantic way but in a sullen dead dog kind of way.

"That sucks. I remember when we met that guy. It was at your sisters' party."

"I remember." She doesn't smile but anyone could see the rush of energy that jumped into her face. It's a memory. "We were all so wasted we talked about bullshit till like six in the morning."

Gordon nods thoughtfully as he takes the last drag off of the beer he's holding tosses it aside and grabs another. She looks at him recollecting more than that individual memory but all the times he's been there to listen to her prattle on about the nuances of her life, all the times they met after work and watched television while passing a bottle of liquor between them. The haze of drunken reasoning she exists in right now draws a simple conclusion she would never come to sober. Glossed over and inundated with alcohol she can easily tell that she should have been dating Gordon the whole time. All those flirty fleeting moments that burnt out were wasted opportunities. Doors of perception unperceived.

Gordon reaches deep inside his faded black pants and pulls out a pack of Menthol flavored cigarettes. Before he can take one out and light it Audrey addresses him.

"When do you think your going to die?"

"I don't know."

"Do you think about it?"

"Off and on I guess. Why? Do you have it planned out?" He finish's the statement tugging a single cigarette out of the pack and clumsily places it on the exterior of his mouth.

"Don't smoke now." Audrey lunges at Gordon and in a halfmoment she hold his cigarette between her hands. She attempts to grab and run but he throws a tight grip around her hips and pulls her closer.

He does his best to reach around her grabbing desperately at the menthol, that's always out of reach. Eventually she spins around to face him grinning with child-like excitement.

They plunge into each other like it was planned, almost as if it was marked on a calendar for months in anticipation. It's not a hard, grabby, touchy, Cinemax kiss but a casual rush forward. A puzzle piece dropped into place. Gordon knows how finite her intentions are but he doesn't pull back. If he could he'd do this every day. She doesn't stop the embrace either it just ends on its own, expiring. After it does Audrey looks into his eyes again. Stroking his bald, shaved head and working all the way down his broad tough neck.

"Gordon there's so much we have to do before we die."

"What do you have in mind?" His big hands gently comb over her firm welcoming posterior while her thin stout arms tighter around his waist. She just looks down into the fire and talks.

"I just don't want to be thinking about the things I've done, the things we've done and regret them." Gordon pivots shifting his body so he can look directly into the fire with her. He throws his right arm around her shoulder and pulls her tight speaking softly into her ear.

"Anyone who has common sense will remember that the bewilderments of the eyes are of two kinds, and arise from two causes:

either from coming out of the light or from going into the light. This is true of the mind's eye, quite as much as of the physical; and he who remembers this when he sees any one whose vision is perplexed and weak, will not be too ready to laugh. He will first ask whether that soul of man has come out of the brighter life, and is unable to see because unaccustomed to the dark, or having turned from darkness to the day is dazzled by excess of light."

"What the fuck does that mean?"

"Your life is so dope it's blinding you and later on you'll realize it." She shakes her head disapprovingly.

"I don't think it's that at all."

"Maybe not, either way we should dance." He clutches her hand inside his and extends his arm straight out taking a tango position.

"I don't know how to dance this way." He turns his head his facial structure changes into a serious pallet of concentration. "Gordon there's no music!"

"Who cares?" He doesn't know how to tango either instead he swings her around wildly until she screams and even after that. She settles into the maddening activity closing her eyes and spinning. The two never step on the menthol cigarette now shining a dying ember up at the scene. Right around this time Steve and Ben finally convince Walter to shut off the game.

Still Fat

Everyone in the office was wrapped up in Todd's overactive sweat glands. In work environments sometimes there are anomalies like the shy hooker or the garbage man who vomits instantly at the onset of a bad smell, situations that make you wonder what they were thinking when they took the job.

"Fuck you! The fucking ad said it was only a free fucking sample no strings attached. THE FUCKING AD SAID NO STRINGS ATTACHED! I call in and get conned into buying the crap and it doesn't work. I want my money back or I'm going to see my lawyer!"

His co-workers on each side are catching everything out of the corner of their eye. The customer's genuine rage projects outside of the earpiece and out into work place, too powerful to be contained.

Beside him an emaciated man with pale skin and red hair chuckles and turns to a group of his associates. Todd's mind wanders into the pool of possible jokes they are creating in his image. The sweaty gland man who can't handle himself on the phone. Why doesn't he just jump off a bridge?

Todd is fat but he's also nervous and being nervous is worse then being fat. Nothing is worse then being both. A lot of the people that work around him are at that age where teenager meets real human being and in his opinion they are not dealing with the transition very well. His forehead is breeding thick beads of salt water that are falling down into his eyebrow before he can wipe them off.

"Sir, I want to…"

He wasn't going to let Todd speak for too long. "Fucking vultures man! You fucking upsold me to automatically ship this crap to me for months and charge me an arm and a leg. You guys took advantage of me because I'm trying to get better and you saw an opportunity to make money off my problems. You should be ashamed how you treat your customers."

The first thing Todd learned from his new boss Danielle is that "Customer" is the most ridiculous term in the human language. The word carries some special connotation that equates to deserving of favors and just because someone does a transaction with us does not give them special relevance. New Marketing Solutions values profit, then employees, then last comes customers. The importance in a customer is only their profit to the company not their feelings. Danielle was very straight forward about this.

This customer has traveled the same frustrating process as so many others. Two rooms away is a large open calling bay where a loose knit group of traveling phone mercenaries are cobbled together to receive inbound calls responding to specifically worded and carefully placed advertisements. The mercenary explains how the wording in the ad might be tricky and that you will get a free sample, upon the purchase of the product. The sample is in addition to your first purchase.

People have problems that you have to isolate and utilize to sell the product. Are you bald, bad skin, small boobs? Somehow you don't match up to what you perceive ideal people to look like and we have the cream (or pill) that can get you there. Todd spent some time on his first day just sitting with a cup of coffee, off to the side of the bay and watching. They were all so good. That was the problem.

This customer called Todd after he had shaken off the hypnosis of the perfect sale and taken the pill, to no avail. Todd went through the basic steps. "Sir, are you supplementing the pill with a reasonable diet and exercise program? The packet clearly states…" The customer was not impressed with this explanation. He ripped into Todd again with vicious terminology you tend to save for someone you know well who has betrayed you in some way. Todd was a customer service agent but his job has more in common with a soccer goalie.

"Sir there is no reason to use that kind of vocabulary!" To his left a tiny blond woman in acid wash jeans tries not to laugh at him. Todd can hear Danielle's high heels behind him.

People have a short leash at this company. Turn over is massive, there is a psychological profile you either meet or don't last. The blond next to him is a very kind person who gives a lot of her check to charity but is absolutely unrelenting and vicious on the phone.

Behind him he hears the click clack of her heels and wonders how he can still be sweating. How does he have moisture left? He lets out a stutter and once he finishes his point, the angry man from Arkansas rails on him again even harder. Todd's tongue starts to feel dry and tired. People get fired here for not having that killer instinct and he knows it. Danielle has a headset on and has no doubt started listening to his conversation.

Todd only knows about Danielle from the lunch room where he still sits alone and eats in his own silence listening to other people talk about anyone and everyone. The red head who was laughing at him now is named Gill and he is very clearly having sex with a manager named Debra from the payment processing division who has known Danielle for years. She gushed as she laid out the details for Gill. Debra wears a wedding ring but Gill certainly doesn't, Todd took notice.

Apparently Danielle met her husband when she began dating his girlfriend at the time. He kept a cordial relationship with his ex and he liked Danielle a great deal. No one told Todd the rest. He wasn't sure how many glances were exchanged before the musical chairs occurred. How many seemingly fun gatherings with all parties present pervaded before the itch became too much for the both of them. Only Danielle could tell that part of the story. NMS doesn't have an education department or a binder to give to new employees, it just has Danielle. From the time you first start until you are either trained up to speed or fired she dictates what happens in the customer service area. It's a strange journey to depend on her to such an extent, come to grips with her kindness only and then meet her history through unkind whispers.

She used to be so nice she got in trouble. You can't be too nice in a room of mercenaries and their keepers so the years had cooled her substantially. Closer to forty years old then she would ever admit, she dresses like a professional woman who wants to be noticed. Every day for the first week he worked there he would hear a new story from someone about a different employee she had slept with. They say she had stalked some of them but Todd didn't believe that. So many people throw out the word stalker like it's a funny word for someone they had sex with who now wants an actual relationship.

Now she wasn't a rumor, she wasn't a woman aging well who looked real good in a black mini-skirt. She was behind him and she might fire him.

From behind him she called out over the click clack of her heels. "Put him on hold."

"Sir, I'm going to have to put you on hold!"

"Why are you putting me on hold?" The man from Arkansas fumed and suspected the worst.

"I want to see what I can do about this situation." He begrudgingly agreed. At this point everyone had stopped the chuckling because Danielle had taken a deadly interest in the conversation. You don't laugh when it gets to that level.

Todd swiveled around in his chair with a wet collar soaked in neck sweat, his armpits were utterly unmentionable.

"Tell him he's still fat." Her jet black hair rested casually on her shoulders her arms folded underneath her breasts.

"Why?"

"He needs to lose weight, we can do that. We can give him another free 3 months and see how it goes. If it does start to work we can discount future shipments based on the trouble he has had."

"Oh, ok." He was about to swivel back around when she put out her hand on his arm rest and held him there for a second.

"One thing: don't let him control this call. If he yells you yell back, you are being too professional." The click clack started again with her continuing the pacing that she started when she noticed the call was out of hand.

Todd put on his headset "Sir."

"Yes."

"I'm back. I think you have a problem Henry."

"You people are my problem!"

"No, you are still overweight Henry. You called us to get rid of the weight that is going to cost you years of your life. You're carrying around extra weight that weakens your heart and gives you a lot of negative medical conditions."

"How FUCKING DARE YOU…"

"HENRY! Listen to me! I don't want to refund you the money and have you die of high blood pressure. I want to help you solve this thing!" He was louder now then before but still sweating like Norman Fell in a sauna.

"Why the fuck should I believe anything you say?" There is no such thing as silence on a phone. When Henry from Arkansas fell quiet and let that quiet exist he was still communicating. Sometimes silence means you're nervous and not sure what to say but sometimes it means you're confused and want the other person to speak.

"Look Henry, this shit works. You don't know how many calls we get from people blessing us up and down for this stuff, it works. I want to give you a free three month supply of it. I want you to exercise and eat less. Going forward we'll give you a 50% discount for future supplies, we are sorry for your trouble. Sometimes the body takes time to adjust and everyone's body is different. I wish I could do more but this is what I can do."

No words from Henry is evidence that a hole is being pounded through the wall of aggression he put up.

"What the fuck else can I do."

Todd doesn't respond verbally but nods in agreement.

"Fine. Send it."

"Thank you Henry you have a good day."

The phone conversation ended there. Todd wiped the last of his own juices off his forehead and took off his headset tossing it down on the table authoritatively. As he stood up Danielle was right in front of him with a warm cheap smile.

"Good job Todd!" It's what teachers used to tell him when he did a good job in art class or remembered his change of clothes for Phys ed.

"Could I take a break?"

"Sure."

Their calling center is on the third floor with two other companies. Todd went down all the stairs not in attempt to smoke, he doesn't smoke, but to breathe real air. As he got up the blonde next to him waited a few seconds and followed.

The air helped his skin breath. The sun knew nothing about cheating people of their money and talking them down after, it just shined. The grass wanted him to stay and skip the rest of his day. He sat for a minute on the grass and watched the cars drive by with no knowledge of what he had just done. Henry wasn't in any of those cars. Maybe they were just like Henry and had problems, problems big enough to spend whatever it takes? Todd shook his head.

"You ok?"

Todd made a sound that is best described as an inquisitive grunt and turned around. He tried to think of her name but decided he didn't know it. "I'm ready for the next call."

She looked surprised.

"In a few minutes."

She laughed and pulled a white cigarette with a green strip around its body to her mouth. "My name is Liz."

"Hi. I'm Todd." She nodded quickly as if to say yes I know.

"You did good, was that your first call?"

She was bright and genuine in her conversation; her face was so close to perfect god really might have made it in her image. Todd didn't get it until he looked straight at her and realized how rich the blueness of her eyes are. How alive her cheeks are when she smiles and how much she smiles. It didn't seem to make sense with savage woman who used NO like a swear word or a sword. She stuck right through people who needed help until they bled hope all over the phone lines and it didn't bother her. It never bothered her. "My first real bad one."

She took a long drag and nodded, her hair looked like it could have been bleached or it could be real, maybe it was the light but it was on the border between the two.

"I know I shouldn't feel bad, but I do."

The bright face tightened up at the sides as the smile left and lips got thin for a second. "Shit, feel bad while you can. I wish I could feel bad. I feel bad watching you cause I know I used to feel the same way and I don't anymore. That nerve is gone. Do you know what I mean?"

"Not yet."

"We should go in."

Todd got up from the grass slapping it off of his nice work pants and went back up the stairs slower this time. Slow enough so she would stay behind him and as he hit the door he turned back and spoke loud enough for her to hear.

"You know Liz is a beautiful name." At least he thought it was on her. The sun didn't last that much longer after Todd's call, it went down early even at this time of year.

A reasonably sized ice box is on the edge of a wooden table in George's room filled exclusively with sixteen ounce store bought orange, apple, and cranberry juices. The ice inside is melting gradually changing the position of the juice's the sound of the slushy movement is present in the room.

A hotel is not home it is merely another night alone. George tried to write a poem about how much traveling to different places, staying in moderately priced hotels was not fulfilling he never got past that line but only because he loved it so much. That line said it all, it was really a marvelous simple poem, a sentence long.

At that moment he was trying to draw a mouse in a Musketeer costume sword fighting, although he is unsure what the mouse should be fighting. He's never been good at drawing cats so he draws a large monstrous fish pirate with a massive cutlass ready to bring it down on the Mouseketeer's skull. The fish pirate is a victim of antiquated fight tactics. A cutlass is too bulky and every swing takes its toll on the muscles in your arm. The mouse knows this and that's why he carries a rapier with a long thin blade that he jams in the fish pirate's black heart.

It's a good picture and fairly representative in George's mind of the natural struggle to survive. He decides to take a break and watch some television getting up from the uncomfortable wooden chair to flop lazily on the bed. He is short so the bed seemed endless. He stretched his boney fingers in desperate search for a pillow and pulled it under his long crooked neck. He rubbed the flesh that covers his wrists feeling a little of the pain he'd acquired at the keyboard over the years. The remote control was on the bed where he left it, a television with limited possibilities, just the basic channels and nothing more.

Thirty minutes slipped away in a haze of local news, sit-com reruns, and music videos with plot lines and character actors playing the artists love interest. If George had thought about it he would remark on how vain the world is but he didn't. He was still thinking about how gallant the mouse was that had the last laugh on that foolish fish pirate. Being clever could go a long way he thought and smiled watching the television but paying it no attention.

Like the crashing of a car into a tree a hard knock came at his door. It was a single knock, hard and fast that damn near shook George out of his skin. Slowly, his movements pregnant with fear brought him as close to the door as he was willing to go and he asked the knock,

"What is it?"

The response came immediately in a rushed tone, a man's voice. "I need your help."

The quick desperation inside the words left him no choice. George rolled his neck listening for the crackling and put on a fake smile. When he felt himself ready he gingerly twisted the knob and pulled six inches before stopping and peeping outside.

The man was probably five foot eleven two hundred and fifty pounds he had that look on his face like he could turn from dinner guest to mad dog in less then five seconds. He was wearing a silk shirt so large and ugly it looked like Liberace's tent draped over him. One of the man's big bear hands was being run through his hair to pat it down into some shape the other was clutching tightly to the hand of a woman. George looked at her for only a moment then held eye contact with the huge stranger. He didn't want to look too long at her because in that second he saw her he knew what type of woman she was. She was a passionate woman who stroked the man's Hulk Hogan shoulder's and kissed at his puffed sagging cheeks even as he attempted to greet George.

"Hey man, we really got to get out of here do you have some money for a taxi?"

George simply said "Yes, I do." and slammed the door in his face asking for no part in all this weirdness. He just wanted to be alone, to watch tv and sleep, to draw pictures and write poetry so succinct it could fit in a fortune cookie. He walked over to the icebox and remarked at his shortage of good Orange Juice as he pulled the last Tropicana from its co-habiting juices. After twisting the top and sneaking in one long lustrous sip the knock came again.

It was the same boldfaced knock from the same bull-faced man George was sure of it. He opened the door sharply this time with snide words already in his mind, excuse me sir you asked me if I had money enough for a taxi and I answered you. If you had asked for some money that would be different. That sir was your one question and I have much to do, yes paperwork and orientation in the morning I can no longer entertain silly questions. George was sure that speech would stunt the big dope but as the door gave way to the outside he saw her instead.

She giggled uncontrollably upon seeing him her eyes glazed over and distracted. He looked down and saw her tight brown Velour pants and heard the sound she made on the carpet as she shuffled her feet. She spoke gently but held each word until it burst out.

"Hello sir, my name is Carmen I'm sorry if we interrupted you were just really in a bad situation and need your help." George could easily tell the man to leave without any trepidation but Carmen was interesting, with a strange energy and very attractive. He really couldn't justify his decision in any way but he let her in his room and let her motion the bull-faced man in the sweaty silk shirt inside as well.

Her hair was obviously dyed blonde her lips full and supple, her body appeared to be lithe and lively which is why the big oaf held her so tightly, drawing from the endless heat she gave out. She introduced the bull-faced man as Michael and asked if she could have some apple juice stating with some humor that the beverage's they were drinking did not hydrate them. Even before George agreed Michael tossed her one and took another for himself. He sucked it down like a great beast and hurled it into the corner. To his credit he reached out his hand and offered thanks.

"Thanks for the drink sir it's much appreciated." George shook the man's hand almost not hating the smell of his stink. The stink of sex came from both of them. At first it was sickening but now he almost felt that two utterly strange people smelling of each other's body fluids was pretty darn romantic.

As she got up from the bed shuffling her feet on the rug and easing towards the door she sees the picture, the valiant mouse getting the best of the ragged fish pirate. Her brow furrows and she asks him in that slow flirty erotic voice "Did you do this?"

He nods his head acknowledging his work but thinking about his sudden lack of juice and need for fresh ice. It looked to be a long evening.

"I like it..." It sounded as if she wanted to say more but there just wasn't time. Michael's big paw stroked her shoulder and urged her to leave. Before she went though she ran suddenly up to him as he sat on the bed thinking about juice and sleep and alarm clocks. She kissed him so softly it was barely a kiss and it was odd. Just an amorous goodbye from someone who loved short unfriendly people who could draw. They left as if they disappeared completely, leaving George so deeply stymied it would take the whole night to get his wits about him.

He had no urge for television or juice or ice he just wanted rest. George wanted back the quiet world of solitude he had before Carmen and Michael. He took off his pants and long sleeve shirt occupying a quadrant of the gigantic mattress hoping to sleep all of it off. The touching and feeling, constant sexualized contact they had with each other. Somehow they were as alive in his mind as they were minutes ago they lived in him as the touch of her kiss lived on his cheek.

An hour passed followed by another and he sat up thinking or not so much thinking as still buzzing from the whole experience. The whole thing had left him with too many questions to sleep and unable to focus enough to do anything else. He wondered where they were now, where they were heading. For a while he cracked his knuckles listening to the sickening sound of them pop, he seemed to be a man perpetually sore and exhausted aching at the base of his neck, right above his knees down to the swollen bottoms of his feet. The night had been so strange he had spent far less time thinking about his problems then usual. The more George thought about his problems the more problems he had.

A knock came at the door, this time in succession at a traditional volume. From his bed George sat up quickly and yelled as he had before "What is it?!"

The knock stopped and a man's voice could be heard this time not as boisterous more monotone in a deliberate way. "Hello sir, I am from across the hall and I have something very urgent to discuss." The statement was very formal but hiding something beneath it, a devious undertone.

George thought that maybe this would be the event, the conversation to bookend his evening so he could sleep.

Before he opened the door allowing his new guest in he put on an air of dignified splendor as if he was allowing this person into a palace. He wore a condescending level of grand intention in his appearance and inflection just for fun...to see what reaction he would get. The man who waltzed into the room and greeted George introduced himself as Gilbert and quickly laid out the reason for his visit.

"I was having a party, well not really a party, just a gathering with a few of my friends. I hope we didn't disturb you at all, but anyway some of the guests are missing we are all very worried. I was wondering if you had seen anyone out of the ordinary."

Gilbert possessed an old face with a mean look on it, he was not old but looked as if he had been dissatisfied for so long it made him look that way. He was in all white, crisply starched pants that led down to solid black patent leather shoes. His jacket was double breasted it even had white buttons. The muscles in Gilbert's face were stretched almost to exhaustion trying to avoid any expression of anger. This man was not telling the full story and George did not feel like telling him anything.

"I would love to help you but I haven't heard anything and I really do have a full schedule tomorrow so I must be going to sleep."

George let the words drift from him effortlessly still thinking of himself as the emperor of this hotel room, with no time for the man in the nice white suit. After he finished his brief response Gilbert's face began to turn red slowly as if he was turning into the wolf man. Gilbert balled up both fists and turned away from George for a minute. After that minute George expected to be killed, ripped to pieces in his own hotel room like that poor woman in Psycho. He would never know why.

Another minute went by with Gilbert's chin resting on his chest his fists balled knuckles white, a brilliant seething anger emitted from him and George began to think. He was hoping that if the man chose to bloody his suit with parts of George, to destroy him that it would come all at once like a bug in a bug zapper.

When that minute passed Gilbert pulled his chin high in the air and spoke, guarding each sound as he made it. "Sir, one of the missing patrons is my wife....and another is the man who...well...a man is fucking my wife. That man left the party with her while I was unavailable to stop him. His name is Michael Germain and her name is Carmen Booth. I would like to have come here under different circumstances but this is what my life has become. She's done this before but never like this, never with someone...a mutual friend. If you haven't heard anything then I will leave you to the good night's sleep that will not be mine but...if you are for some reason...leaving something out..." He never finished his sentence it just drifted for a while until the silence killed it.

George shrugged his shoulders giving his condolences for the unfortunate luck the man was having but restated that he had no idea where his wife was. He did this several times each time shrugging his shoulders and wishing him the best all the while hinting at the man to leave, referencing a packed day of orientation just hours away.

Gilbert was unreceptive at first but eventually apologized for the time he had taken up and the improper tone he had taken with him. George waved him away urging that if roles were reversed he would be in a bad way as well. Secretly he feared that if Gilbert found the two lovers he would ruin his nice white suit and possibly her form fitting velour pants. He would tear them limb from limb or Michael would do in Gilbert. Either way it was not a story for a man like George to be involved in.

Gilbert never stopped to look at the picture of the mouse cleverly besting the fish pirate he walked right out the door focused on other things. George crawled under his covers thinking...that perhaps the whole thing is over with.

Chapter II

Well creased tan pants held tight with a fresh dark brown leather belt he even buttoned carefully spending some time on the last button, hitching the two ends of his white collared shirt together. On his bed George had laid out his tie and sport coat. The sport coat a perfect neutral tan color not meant to be too daring. The tie was his greatest source of pride. He sucked in a long breath of fresh morning air before artfully putting the tie in a half Windsor, the best he's been able to form in the first try. The tie was red but not a deep burgundy or a light tawdry neon it was just right. He got very little sleep and when he did he was troubled by strange dreams, loud noises, paranoid inertia that rattled him. None of this mattered now, he was ready finally and he would blend in seamlessly at orientation showing energy but not desperation, being as good as his co-workers but not standing apart. The ladder of success had too far and steep a fall.

George felt good knowing he could be a cog in this big corporate giant for years and years getting annualized raises of five to seven percent minimizing his risk to near nothing. A life without the fear of financial ruin where he would have health care and retirement benefits. All these thoughts sharpened his actions put life in his step and put last night so very far away from him.

In reality it was only as far as the next room. George opened his door and as he pivoted on his right foot he noticed that the room across the hall had the door broken off, splintered, and yellow police tape lined the whole area around it. A brief glance beyond the yellow tape let George know that humans had bled in that room the night before. That was Gilbert's room, Gilbert with the angry white knuckles and mean face who had warned him to be honest the night before. A sudden rush of urgent fear squeezed George asking him what happened to Carmen? Was that her blood? Was it Michael's...or Gilbert's?

Policemen were casually meandering around the scene like mechanics at a car garage they all looked bored and tired worn down by the logistics of their occupation. He wanted to grab one and shake him silly, he wanted to know what had happened. Instead of pursuing this he followed his natural instinct and quickly rushed off to the elevator and out of the hotel. Now wrapped in a shell of confidence internally he was wrecked, sweating and sure of nothing.

The education room was large with a huge circular mahogany table with name tags on each seat. In the corner on the right of the door was the breakfast layout, muffins, bagels, water, orange juice. George knew by the look of the bagels they were bought in bulk at some grocery store with incredibly low standards for storing food. A bad bagel is an insult. George just grabbed an Orange Juice and sucked it down still shaking slightly but hoping that the acidic vitamin C would somehow give him power.

At thirty three George was the second youngest in the room. The women were early to late forties in power suits with thick shoulder pads he could tell they were the one's who drove the SUV's with the smarmy personalized license plates. They walked in with their own coffee cups, freshly styled hair and enough make-up to hold back time...at least for a few hours. He looked at them and sighed knowing that when they went home they would wash it all off and be as sore as he was from years and years in tiny cramped offices. Some of the men were trying to look quiet collected and as if they were thinking deeply but they weren't. Others were completely disinterested in the training and slouched in their chairs with shirts that weren't ironed they fidgeted like children the woman who ran the conference, orientation, training was a blond who was far too extraverted. She seemed like that woman who grew up without rejection, without anyone to tell her that she should be quiet for a while. Her name was Wanda and for the first fifteen minutes of the meeting she talked about her one eyed Siamese cat Archie who was awful to strangers when they came by he hissed and flexed his fur out at them but he was so loving in small ways to her. It was about her cat and her fiancé and so much else no one in the room would ever remember.

After she had brought everyone up to speed on the details of her existence she went around the room and made them introduce themselves. My name is George I am from Oregon....Ohio it's right outside of Toledo. I've been working in the financial field for a little over ten years. After that there was a short judgmental silence as though he should have been able to end it with "I have two lovely daughters Melinda and Jaime and a wonderful wife Isabelle." When this never came what did were the strange glances from those who thought George was odd.

They all had fleeting thoughts about the short odd man with the hump in the back of his neck, but they forgot he existed when the next man spoke. His name was Andy, Andy with the million dollar smile, tall and suave look, easy to like. George was paying no attention to this part of the day the bulk of the course's information would be displayed around ten o'clock maybe ten thirty till lunch. After lunch would be more schmoozing for about forty five minutes before coming back to the overhead projector for more charts and regulations.

He knew the ebb and flow of the process and navigated through it like a professional looking as absorbed in whatever topic was being discussed as he could, taking comprehensive notes. At the end he approached Wanda telling her only that the hotel was experiencing great difficulty and he had to be moved as soon as possible. She mashed up her face in concern nodding and directing him to the young woman in charge of these things. It turned out he had to meet with several people none of them really knowing who handled it in the end they gave George a form to fill out for reimbursement.

It was four fifty four and the sun was still out , time was left in the day to stop in Rite Aid for pads of paper new pens and juice. He walked by a diner and looking through the window saw a man eating a huge pancake, he looked to be greatly enjoying it. George stopped... remembering how bad hotel food can be he decided to walk through the door anticipating the jingle of the bell attached to the door. It drew the waitresses' attention to him; they were waiting for him to sit in a section so they would know who had to serve him.

As he looked around finding an open booth he could stretch out in, a bald man with a newspaper waved him over. He did it in a completely unconcerned way as he let buffalo sauce drip from his chin onto the plate underneath his face. For no reason at all George sat in the booth across from him wondering what the strange bald man in the rain coat could possibly want.

"Your name is George right?"

"Who...are you sir?" His voice began to tremble, palms sweating.

"My name is Philip Jones I'm investigating a homicide," The man lazily dropped his badge on the table letting the light bounce right off it into George's eyes as he continued "You were in the room next door."

"Yes, I saw that there was some commotion in the next room when I left this morning."

The man looked up at him with bored dull brown eyes before he spoke "Look we have witness's that place the happy couple in your room. If their friends of yours you should help me find them before Gilbert does."

George could do nothing at that point, the memory of that night had possessed him so deeply so fully that he had no other option then to tell the man everything. Every little detail from the beginning but he knew that none of it would help because for all his worry he knew nothing about any of these people. Philip Jones just nodded gave him an occasional look all the time finishing his sandwich. As he finished and wiped his hands free of any mess he finished his comments.

"You probably don't have a real grasp on how damn scary this whole thing is but the man you met last night, the man with Carmen...Michael Germain went back to Gilbert's room while you were asleep and the hotel staff found him dead there. In order for me to explain to you how dangerous Gilbert Booth is I would have to jabber on for a damn bit longer then I wish too. My recommendation is for you to forget about this whole thing and go back to doing whatever you do. If you run into Carmen or Gilbert call me immediately." He handed a card to George that listed his cell phone address and name then waved the waitress over and paid the bill nodding his head pleasantly at George as he left.

The next three days were like years, every hour seemed a full day of looking over his shoulder listening to the sounds of the people walking behind him. George suffered even more then normal feeling more sharply than before the pains above his knees and on the bottom of his feet. His stomach twisted and cramped up, finding a new hotel didn't help in the least, he still felt as if he was being followed.

Pretty soon Wanda was done with the mandatory training, concluding the course by asking the class to give itself a hand. The class felt so good they gave themselves a standing ovation, standing, clapping and leaving promptly with courtesy. George was reimbursed for his hotel stay, but a man died no one could pay for that. Poor Carmen, what would come of her, he wondered?

When he opened the door to his house he was happy, happy that there were no cats no kids no middle aged women in power suits. He was excited to be with unhindered silence again gracefully moving from one room to the next wiping the dust off his kitchen table with a paper towel. Before he thumbed through the mail he brought in with him he turned on the DVD player and television pressing play on the remote control. He knew what movie was in the player. MOONRAKER had always been George's favorite bond film it was big and ridiculous and always cracked him up. Roger Moore was the real James Bond anyway. All of a sudden a letter shook his world he followed each word and trembled slightly.

Dear George,
It has been no small feat tracking you down, this is a very awkward position for a man like me to be in. Your potential involvement in my affairs has cost me dearly I want you to know that she's left me, overreacting to a situation I didn't get a chance to remedy. I often wonder what you discussed in that short span where my life was being pulled apart. A man who was a close friend to me is dead now I have to live with that. You are the clever one who watched us tear each other to pieces enjoying all the excitement without any of the danger.

Always with you, Gilbert Booth

George smiled after reading it knowing that at least he hadn’t found her. She could start over now, and he could finish up the laser fight in space maybe get a good night’s sleep after Roger Moore saved the world.

Capable of Floating

Women buy perfume either expensive or cheap that smells just plain awful. Women shouldn't need a signature smell to lure you in. They aren't bacon. Most people who bathe properly smell how your mind wants them to. She tried like hell to smell like bad wine. I loved the person she covered up in fake smells and hair highlights. I used to dream her during the day just to have her there when she wasn't in the room. She called me stupid.

Ten tons of imaginations don't weigh shit. She kept telling me that I can't live in my dreams that I'll get stranded there and never come back. What she meant to say is that she couldn't come with me. You always have to consider the idea that any relationship will dissolve. Whenever the thought crosses you start to put together a storyline for its demise and how it would fall apart. I've always been right, in the worst way. She's exactly like I feared she would be and so the conversation and the tears were not only the dreadful destruction of the most prized connection I'd had with a person but boring. She had to cry, she had to blame me, then she had to apologize. It's the lackluster process of accepting a newly negative situation and all the changes of emotion are a good way to run from your responsibility in it.

I know what I did. I spent too much time chasing the promises I had made and narrowly escaping contradictions. There is nothing worse than being fooled into hiding who you are. Its not all her fault. No one grows up in the world without expectations that you won't allow yourself to live up to. You have to shatter them and hope the shards don't break and stick inside you. It is my fault that I never said "You should love me even though I'm always going to be someone you never charted a course for. You ended up with me. Do you like it?" I should have forced the issue to her instead of hoping we would both grow into each other.

Sean Hannity calls me stupid every night from 9pm-10 and I still watch. The world doesn't know that I'm a genius for ignoring its insults and loving it anyway. Loving myself regardless.

She made me realize I don't want to just pass through shifts with people; I want to climb to the very top of days. She was always naturally half way there but stuck at a comfortable point. I wanted to be the force that kept her trying…sometimes I wanted to make her.

Laughing can't mask how sad or scared you are. Admitting your scared doesn't make you brave but it keeps you from being foolish. She was fearless.

An ecosystem of little lies told to yourself. A fancy blank teleprompter. Everyone has to do so much more then hug, kiss, and appreciate people we hold dear. We have to hold on to the tired broken ones, the stupid ones who could have genius in them. Even if its only for seconds. She was always too busy to catch my seconds. We were always too busy fighting.

I float back into our best moments whenever life slows down enough for my mind to leave it. I play them in slow motion and kick myself. I'm going to know the great ones are great as they're unraveling next time, before the kiss before the hug. I'm going to smile and keep what we could have had gripped tightly in the deepest chamber of my chest and when I love the next one I'll be perfect. I promise it to you.

Some people teach you enough that they never leave. I'm not going to try and be so grounded that I bury myself. If ten tons of imagination is weightless then maybe I'll just float away and you can meet me there.

Nice Broken People

Before the world had ear buds people stuffed their prehistoric heads into huge head phones with massive cushioning that covered your ears completely. They provided a housed musical environment for Jake and he loved them even though when he was done and took them off his ears they would be covered in sweat.

Radiohead had just put out an album and he remembered back when he cared. He used to walk through Cherokee Park amongst the cyclists and the families playing and nod his head so steadily that dogs being led by their masters would copy his movement. He called all the guys he used to know from the bands he had bounced between for years and they all agreed Amnesiac was crap and everyone missed Pablo Honey and the Bends.

Cherokee park wasn't far away but the nights there are for lovers and druggies and he wasn't either tonight. He was stepping lively to get home while his cd player shouted in his ears letting his hair get slapped around by the wind. He wasn't attending the University of Louisville anymore but that didn't mean he couldn't hang around.

The time was showing on his face even as genuine attempts were made to prevent its loud declaration. He would shave every single day and make sure the black hair held together an island of black on the point of his chin. She hated it.

A woman waved to him beaming approval without thought and he did what he could to return the gesture but they didn't know each other. That's how it is in Kentucky. Some places up east if you're dressed a certain way the elderly will hug the curb and look away hoping you don't mug them. A young man with a leather duster and half gloves walking down a street named by a moron, Longest Avenue, didn't mean anything in Kentucky. She waved at all the strangers, he guessed, just happy to have people in the world to talk too.

The trees were hundreds of years old and the house he was staying in wasn't far behind. It used to be a bright blue that faded into a disgusting used toothpaste white. The old couple they all rented from were very nice but not too good at anything a land lord should know how to do.

The steps were falling apart so he took them all at once. He hit stop at the end of the third time in a row he listened to Anyone can Play Guitar and pulled out his keys.

"It's open."

She was there on the other side of the porch looking right at him. She had been waiting.

"Broken you mean?"

Her shoulders always shrugged so strangely like they weren't meant for it but she insisted on it. If this had been a year earlier he would have walked up to her and held her until she kissed him. He wouldn't have had to wait. He blew out his breath in an exaggerated motion and pushed the cracked wooden door open, not waiting to see if she would come in after him.

They used to fuck but not anymore. She took it much too personal for his liking.

Cassie had been perfect once upon a time though and had a good run at it. He met her in a music class they were both taking for the credits. She felt like a fantasy for six months maybe nine, the type of girl too thick to afford a bad attitude and so she never developed one. Jake never kept women around that long but each time he cut into her and insulted her, every time he used all his power to pull his arms out of her grasp and flee the room she'd follow. Each time she didn't get the hint so he kept raising the stakes by cheating on her but after a while she laughed in his face, asked how it was. If he had to put it in a sentence it would go something like; I thought I knew what I was doing but I had no idea. When they're alone together and can't find anything to say she won't stay with him while he drinks and put him to bed anymore. Now he's stuck with her as a friend and sometimes he likes it. Not sure how much of the time that is.

She did follow him inside.

The creaks were all in the same tone, the stairs, the floors they all gave the same moan. Louisville felt like any other city in spots but where he lives it feels like a trunk in your grandparents basement hidden away and forgotten.

As Jake enters the door he is instantly greeted by a man on the couch waving off a cloud of smoke.

"Fuck Jake. Didn't know it was you. Ever since the door broke I've been suspicious as hell of people busting in and uhhh…" He pointed down at the ash tray.

Jake walked in and leaned over it. "You killed that poor blunt Jim. It's dead."

"Didn't want to get busted man."

"Even if we scrape it, it will never be like it was before you killed it." Jake looked up at Jim for more of an explanation.

"I had it in its prime and…" He got up and walked to the dark white refrigerator and opened it eventually putting his head inside it and continued speaking from there "…I can vouch for its potency and flavor."

"Dick." Jake took off his duster and walked past the living room and into his bedroom throwing it in a heap onto his bead. A smell hit him and he blinked. Why did every room in the house smell like her?

Cassie was back and smirking like she ate the moon and it was made of sharp cheddar. She had a big fuzzy sweater on that made her arms look even shorter and her face look even brighter. Something was different.

"Did you tell him?"

Jim shook his head from side to side and tipped up the Miller high life that was available.

"Can I tell him?"

Jake was not going to allow this he put his arms straight up in the air and moved all his fingers as quickly as he could to distract her. "What the fuck is going on!"

After Jim was done with his quick swig he went back to the couch and looked up at his friend "I got a job."

"Ok." If anyone gave more emotion away through body language then Jake no one in Louisville would ever meet them.

Cassie strolled right by giving the type of walk that showcased her butt and whispered to him as she took a seat next to Jim on the couch. "He's a freelance clown."

"WHAT!!!" His eyes went to the couch, hands to his sides. "Are you kidding me?"

Jim's face looked stupid when he smiled his lips never fully curled just on one side. He always looked like a poor John Wayne imitation. "Not really. There is this place in town that provides inflatable crap for kids birthday parties and they just decided to try and provide…clown service as well. They need people."

She calls it out as it comes to her and it hits so hard she makes sure she gives it vocal personality "Do you have any experience? I mean do you have any idea what you will be doing?"

"I'll figure it out. How hard is it to make little kids laugh?" Jim was either naturally calm or stoned and neither Cassie nor Jake knew which. Some people get stoned so long they are stoned, they think slower, make every motion in stages, and are predisposed to sitting around and sharing odd embarrassing stories. Jim fit all criteria but the haunting suspicion hit you quite quickly in his presence that without the drugs he might be the very same person.

Jake had been staring at the Miller high life Jim was walking around and it looked good enough to leave the clown discussion altogether and get his own from the dirty fridge. Not much was inside of it but beer, cheese, and deli meat in different stages of use. They relied on Cassie to stock good enough food to take advantage of but she had caught on. She already paid most of the rent for the place and there was no need to push her on getting new food and test her resiliency. Neither of them wanted her to leave and only one knew why.

With the beverage clutched tightly Jake pulled his hand out and came to a conclusion, all at once.

His voice was rabid with volume "Do either of you know what this means?"

The two seated parties were silent until he declared his realization.

He popped the top and started a light shimmy with his shoulders not knowing that his windblown hair was doing the same dance atop his head. "I am the sex machine!"

"Fuck you! No way!" Jim piped in but was drowned out.

"We've known each other since Junior High. Do you know what they used to call us?" He looked to Cassie and her eyebrows said I have no clue. "They used to call Jim and I the flannel brothers and nearly every girl in our age group in this area woke up on one day of her life with our dry semen in her lady cavern wondering where we went."

"Lady cavern?" Jake smiled at her. He loved disgusting her. "Is that the best you could come up with?" The smile went from grape to raisin.

"All the girls that wanted the boisterous guy, the creative one who could give them a good time would come to me and all of their friends…who hated me…thought I was slime…they still thought Jim was the nice one. The one with the good intentions." Some people can become so happy that it's frightening. Jake does it a lot. He gets wrapped up in himself, while he's talking his internal narrative takes each thought further and eventually you can see in his toothy grin the images he's not sharing and you want to throw up, just a little. "But I'm telling you now old boy….Baby Baby I got the feeling…Baby baby baby…baby baby baby…" He stopped talking and began grunting and dancing in the middle of the living room like a child simulating a Native American dancing and a train chugging along at the same time.

Jim was a little bit taken aback by the show but not without words. "I'm not becoming a priest. I'm still going to be knee deep in…action." Jim caught himself and changed the last term before it came out. He hadn't taken on the adversarial relationship with Cassie that Jake had and didn't really have any interest in replicating it.

"Are you kidding?!?!?! You can't get no damn pussy! How long does it take in conversation with a woman before she asks what you do? You're going to lie every time? Hide your big ass shoes and squeaking nose?" Cassie did laugh at that image, something about it hit her the right way and her face got really red while she pulled off the combination laugh-cough-lost control move.

"You're fucked up. You wish you could get rid of me and get a bigger slice of the future freshman. That's the only reason you join any of these stupid bands so you can win over dumb college chicks with that line-I'm in a band-I don't even need that crutch you know. I'll tell the girl to her face. I'm a clown for hire, I'll fuck you, change your life, then make your little brothers birthday the best he's ever had. That is the next level."

Just as Cassie was getting herself together this statement hit and was even funnier. She waved in the air to signal the conversation should be paused, they thought it was so she could catch her breath but she was more worried things would get funnier and she would urinate in her underwear. With this conversation anything was possible.

Both men looked dumbstruck and finally dumped their focus on her, Cassie the one who could press any given spot on Jake and have him in her bed again tonight.

Finally her face was getting back to a normal color and the tears in her eyes were wiped away. "Look. I fucked both of you. Neither of you are that big a deal."

You could feel the air escape through the windows and vents and a lot of it was filled with confidence. Cassie was never afraid to do that. Jake's face pursed up as he responded "She's just talking shit. She had her time."

"Right. I speak from experience." Their eyes met for a minute and the connecting area between them wasn't filled with the remains of affection but that spark of hate that love tumbles into and gets stuck in. "Who told either of you that you were sex machines."

Jim was looking down at the coffee table and pulling the label off of his beer. "It was just a…joke...James Brown song we both like…its stupid." Jim was at his most appealing to Cassie when he was this uncomfortable and vulnerable. You could never make Jake vulnerable he would push you down flights of stairs before he got there. Her face changed and her right hand tip toed around his neck and shoulder beginning to physically pull him tighter.

He didn't want to dance anymore. Not when they started this. He went in his room and turned on the stereo. Making sure James Browns 20 greatest hits was on the right track and he played it loud enough for everyone to care.

Jake called as many whores as it took to get one for the night. His voice was different for each one some of them needed him to speak low and soft some preferred his tone deep and rugged. He was going to bring one of them home and be real public about it to teach both of them a lesson but by the time he found a skinny blond with bad enough lipstick the two of them were gone watching the moon. Off in Cherokee Park somewhere.

Jake had those moments with her but he didn't have to have the moon as an excuse. They used to have each other wherever they went irrepressibly trying to get out of public as soon as they could so no one could watch and that kind of magnetism, they don't have. Jake spent that night bullshitting a little girl who believed him but his mind wasn't with her even when the rest of his body was.

He doesn't live there anymore but still hangs out with Jim every week. They don't really talk about her and if Jim starts to Jake ignores him and talks over the subject laying a different one over it. It was a while ago when Jake threw away all her pictures but people are better then pictures they stick in your skull until you think you've forgotten them and then they come back. Bolder then the frozen moment she's a mixed emotional imprint of everything he loves and wants to hate. He remembers that she had a lot of good butt jeans and great big boobs, she could hold you like no one else existed in the world and all Jake has left is freedom. He has the discipline to never let himself think of her personality unless it's a bad thing. That way he can curse her stupid face. It's a whole lot better than missing it.

Goodnight Dad

In the open field the fog descends on George. Moisture inundates not just him but the leaves of grass filling them and washing them over with drops of moisture still left over from the rain. He shakes briefly trembling at the sudden coolness. The fog walks through him and around him until he is its hostage. Touching lightly the white hairs under his nose he sniffles a bit pulling back at the scared mucus in his nose. His skin braces having lost its rosy color in the chill of evening. Rotting wood lays about with insects huddling in it for warmth. All the insects without tribal security are already dead at the helm of the season but some survive, quietly.

He cups his hands to his mouth and breaths hot air into his hands letting it not only echo inside his palms reflecting new warmth but letting the air escape back onto him for a split second before it dies. Inexplicably he begins to hum so low that not even the wind would hear him, he begins it with his mouth do...do do do My funny valentine sweet comic valentine...do do do do...with this he loses track of the swaying grass and the deep fog and the temperature being twenty degrees colder then the day before. He doesn't dance to his own tune but sways a bit humming the sound of the words.

"Dad...what are you doing out here? I told you about coming out here alone!" The voice is careful, loving and sharp stewed together in unified purpose. The words jump over his right shoulder covered with the confounding fog.

"I know. I'm sorry." George doesn't move or hum he just opens his great brown eyes as wide as he can onto the rotting log with the bugs in it and the frozen stream beside it. "This is a great backyard you know."

"I know Dad, come on inside." Her hand lightly lands on his shoulder blade almost a petting motion, close to an embrace. So close that he finally turns around, looking at his feet to make sure he's not stepping in any mud or treading on anything important.

He looks up at her sharp nose, her mother's nose. Her eyes are a distant brown that matches the hair dye she uses these days. She has a tattered grey sweatshirt on over an immaculate blue dress. It flows out of the bottom of the sweatshirt bounding onto the blades of green grass, without tarnish. After a short look he makes an odd face and gives a light punch to her shoulder.

"Let's get back to your party, Kim." She forces a smile and trudges laboriously back to the house as close to George as she can be without them touching, as silent as they can be without lacking affection for one another.

Under his breath he lets the beat continue do...do do do My funny valentine you make me SMILE with my heart...do do do...his pace begins to speed up until he is off the grass all together and pulling open a screen door that moans a dreadful creak. He holds it open for Kim who scurries through it with vigor leaving nature to its silent frigidity.

The home is 2,150 square feet two car garage 2.5 bathrooms which just means you can piss in all three but shower in only two. It has three bedrooms and a pool in the back big enough to need a pool boy. These days it's too cold for the pool, the water was emptied out weeks ago when the bitter cold was simply a rumor.

George enters into a kitchen with chatter echoing through it voices layering over each other. Thirty five people all in small groups, different stations in the house in tight formations talking and then waiting to talk after the response is finished. Only one person recognizes their entrance, and he skips over abandoning conversation with another woman to run over.

He has a red cardigan that adheres closely to a white collared dress shirt. He's pulled the collar so it hangs over the neck hole of his sweater. He looks at George only after he has wrapped his arms around Kim acknowledging him as an afterthought.

"Where were you guys?" His locks of curly brown hair dance on his head as he looks to Kim.

"Daddy was in the backyard again." As she orates her eyes open large at the man, she embraces him around the chest.

"Any wine here Abe?" George looks down at the floor that is speckled with fragments of sand and dirt. He looks over at the doorway noticing how clean the welcome mat is in comparison to the floor.

Abe in the red cardigan comes to life pointing with a long finger over to a bottle of wine with an obese man on the front. It's called Fat Bastard wine. George walks over to the bottle trying to steer himself between the bold body movements of Kim's friends. Some of them are so eager to switch talking partners that they would shoulder check the good time right out of George if he wasn't careful.

George is careful and finally gets to the bottle pouring the deep red wine into his glass until it is enough.

"George!" From behind the voice digs its hooks into the air.

"Jeremy, how are you?" After filling his glass George turns around to a chubby short man with an untucked bright blue dress shirt and pants on that are much too large for him. The man has a smile on his face that could last for hours, days, or presidencies.

"I got a question for ya George." To this George nods his head taking the first sip of Fat Bastard "Do you think Joshua Fry Speed was gay?" George stops to arch his brow, silent for a minute.

"Who is Joshua Speed?"

"He was Lincoln's BEST friend. Carl Sandburg said their relationship had 'streaks of lavender' get this I hear they slept in the same bed together for FOUR years. I don't know what those streaks of lavender were but that's some crazy stuff? I mean you don't just sleep in the same bed with a dude. Some people are like 'those were different times' that's a bunch of bologna. He might have been a meat smuggler."

"Damn Jeremy didn't Lincoln have four children?"

"Yeah yeah...and Cary Grant was married a bunch of times too but who's that fooling? If he's bisexual that's even crazier. Picture a bisexual president during a time of civil war just taking a piece of everything he can get. That's messed up. Speed and him apparently kept in contact their whole life. Some real Brokeback Mountain style stuff. Brokeback Lincoln. That's kind of funny."

George sucks greedily at the rest of his wine with no time to taste it. When he has emptied it he goes back to the bottle giving himself more. George trembles a minute until he gets halfway through the second glass and finds again the rhythm to My Funny Valentine in his head.

Jeremy pushes past George and yells "Where is the music in this BITCH!!!" to which a resounding laugh erupts and circulates. Seizing the moment Jeremy does a little shuffle adding some arm movements he remembers from Saturday Night Fever. A woman named Rebecca joins him in the dance shaking her hips laughing while she dances with her pointer fingers up toward the ceiling. Jeremy does a Jazzersize grapevine behind her sizable caboose and begins to do a mock pelvic thrust. The only music that drives them is the cheers of their friends, the chuckling of the many.

George watches this for a moment deciding this is a great time to empty the second glass. Hoping that by the third he should feel that warm power. Shaking his head he thinks about the warm summer months drinking wine with his friends in the backyard. He thinks about Paul (who is very ill) and Rachel (who see's him on Sunday's to study torah). He spends a lot of time standing with his third glass and traveling backward rather than merely remembering. He travels to those moments and feels the feelings again sometimes different feelings, sometimes he acts in a different way. Each time is unified by the potency of the experience the power of the people involved. That must be why they stick.

The same light touch comes to George's shoulder again and it trembles just as before, but before the cold caused the tremble. Her voice arcs shooting words into his ear as he finishes the third glass.

"You okay Daddy?"

He shrugs and looks up at her reaching into his pockets past the lint and wrapping his fingers around a metal object until it is in the base of his palm. "I'm getting a little tired, I might take a nap." She nods at him with red rosy cheeks and dark eyebrows and that sharp nose. "I want to give you your present first though." From his pocket it comes presented to her and dropped into her hand from a tight fist that unleashes it.im looks at it for a moment feeling around it with familiarity but modest familiarity. She knows it's a metal hand open with a huge eye in the middle, she turns it over and see's the Hebrew characters etched together in rows. Her fingers run down and across each row slowly "What do they mean?"

"It's the travelers' prayer; this Chamsa will guard you from the evil eye. It carries with it The Travelers prayer." George mumbles it speaking more sharply with his hands as she looks at no one and listens only to him, "*'May it be Your will, Lord, My God and God of my ancestors, to lead me, to direct my steps, and to support me in peace. Lead me in life, tranquil and serene, until I arrive at where I am going. Deliver me from every enemy, ambush and hurt that I might encounter on the way and from all afflictions that visit and trouble the world. Bless the work of my hands. Let me receive divine grace and those loving acts of kindness and mercy in Your eyes and in the eyes of all those I encounter. Listen to the voice of my appeal, for You are a God who responds to prayerful supplication. Praised are You, Lord, who responds to prayer.'* It was your mother's."

George leans in taking advantage of the silence and gives her a soft kiss on the forehead. A soft kiss that freezes her in time, and with that he is gone, taking powerful steps up stairs coated with carpet. Kim pictures him smiling on the way up.

The Badge

If there really is a devil there's a little bit of him in me without a doubt. I feel him in my trachea when I address the customers. After I give them a big hearty hello and start describing what a new credit card can do for them that moment comes where you wait for a hang-up. You wait for the phone to click you prepare for the next call. I feel him when that silence is followed by a question; we call it a buying sign something like "well how much does it cost?" or "What's the rate on this thing?" he must help me begin the show and change the octave of my voice to accommodate the individual liking of that customer. Mirror the call. Without him how could I tell someone whose eighty-five years old that they need a new credit card to help "diversify their finances" help manage their money?

I get that little evil sales tingle that runs through me and I can't wait to do it! It's me versus them and when I get a yes their on the books daddy! Then I remember why I'm standing still in the purgatory that lies between the outside world and the building waiting for a security guard. I forgot my badge. Damn!

The badge that dangles uncomfortably from the old clip they gave me years ago is lost. It's at my house somewhere amongst papers, aluminum cans, and cd's lost in a spiraling shit hole that is my apartment. I will find it eventually but I can't tell this to the security guard. He's a very short man named Ron whose ex military and a big fan of personal responsibility. If nobody has a badge, if we just forget about them isn't that a slippery slope that leads to complete anarchy? No, it isn't but I'm not going to argue the point, I see him slide into the little booth where I've been waiting. All the security guards wear green jackets, it adds to his classic 70's cop mustache and jovial yet stern demeanor that he uses to temper discipline but it's obvious how he is going to approach me and I have anticipated the whole speech.

"HEY! Where's your badge buddy?" He shakes his head dramatically pursing his lips and continues "You can't go losing that you know how much those things are worth…" It lasts a few seconds that are a century I'll give him anything just to stop, I just wait for him to cease and slide the clipboard in front of me. Finally he swings his head from side to side giving up and pushes the clipboard towards me like it's a child that needs to be held with consideration. I sign it quickly and grab the sticker that will temporarily take the badge's place. As I place it on my right breast he pushes the button opening the door looks me square in the face and says "Dave…you'll have it tomorrow right?"

I'll have the badge or flee the country; I'll beg your forgiveness! I just want to go to work, solicit the elderly and linger till the shift ends. The end seems so far from now. "No problem, Ronnie!"

I come through the door and see the hopelessly nice middle aged woman who works at the desk she greets me like were old friends, I wave and smile but its all artificial. I swing by my manager's spacious office, I see his feet first their kicked over the desk, the prick has forgotten his badge three times this week. He's got a big hulking athletic body but he smirks and lays about like a bored child. He's a big goof whose job it is just to make sure we sit and call, he doesn't have to remember his badge. As a member of the bourgeoisie management class the security guards can trust him, knowing that a man whose achieved enough to have his own office must know where his badge is. The bloated ugly proletariat will forget their badge and when they do they must be disciplined. My manager's name is Clark and he has a sickeningly slick way of addressing me.

"Dave, it's not like you to lose your badge." JESUS, maybe I've changed; everyone is telling me that I have. Maybe I've turned some kind of corner and I'm on a path to self-destruction I don't have my badge I don't even know where it is!

I just shake my head with a serious look on my face playing into the concept that I am a poor lost soul incomplete without my badge. It allows me to sneak by and nestle into my cubicle, I finally get to login to the dialer. I love the stability and rhythm of calling on the dialer it's a part of the day where nobody has cancer, nobody wants to talk to me about what I don't have or what I need to have. I just go from call to call in a sincerely peaceful motion soliciting people.

There are some people on my team who I do love. Its not a genuine love because I only love them here but while we are both here we are great friends. Linda has been sitting next to me for a long time and you can't help but love her. She was a forensic examiner for twenty years and developed a sharp sense of humor and brazen attitude doing it. She used to smoke cigarettes and tell jokes over the bodies, she tells me. After a few minutes of continuous calls, to people who are not in or warn against me leaving a message on their voicemail message she peeks over the cubicle wall.

"Hey."

I look up and see her face beaming, something happened. "Hi."

"Do you want to hear a story?" Everyone wants to hear a story that distracts until the next call comes in. Me included. I just nod.

“This guy, I call him and he says he’s tired of the calls and he starts going off…” She waves her hands in the air “…F this and F that and F you until I jump right in and say SIR I’m a nurse during the night, I work two jobs to support my family and one to heal sick people, I don’t need this from you!”

My mind was thrown into a different dimension for a second until I asked “Are you a nurse?”

It was one of those looks she shot me that is in my all time book for feeling stupid. I was as stupid in that second as the guy who stopped yelling.

I nodded my head up and down and finally smiled. “I like it. I have to say I’m a little Jealous.”For the rest of the day we traded secondary occupations back and forth, I was a lobsterman, she worked with the mentally ill, and on and on and on. We had a lot of fun.

I don’t know what being good at this says about me, some people are good at creating medicine for the sick. I’m good at creating the opportunity for poverty, after all what kind of maniac forgets his badge.

Cold White House

TJ had been wary of monsters in the cold white house. At three years old he thought of himself as very adept at sniffing out monsters and would often brag to other children how free of monsters his home in Delaware is.

No one has a better ability to discern the footsteps coming towards their bedroom door then a child. Instantly TJ knew who was on the way and so he leapt into his bed pulling the covers all the way up to the unstoppable dimples in his cheeks. He closed his eyes shut and held them tight.

"TJ" The man walks in wearing khaki cargo pants and a button up dark blue shirt. He speaks slowly.

TJ is silent and doesn't move.

The man walks in and sits at the end of his bed. "What were you doing? I thought you were going to bed?"

His eyes opened just a sliver and he answered in a whisper. "I was looking for monsters."

The man had seen all the same films that TJ had. He'd even watched most of them with him so TJ knew he could trust him with the secret and that he would understand. During careful consideration his eyebrow moved up his head in one solid motion, TJ had his eyes partially closed but all his attention on his guest.

"Where could there be monsters?"

His little fingers had the sheets gripped firmly and with a premeditated caution he slid them down an inch or two to make sure his words were heard. "In the cabinets."

"Monsters can't be in those cabinets TJ." The house is not where anyone lives for too long; it is just a place they use when they visit family. Its not home and when you sleep somewhere big and empty where everything has been painted white and kept new…that's prime monster territory. The man addresses TJ in a matter of fact tone of voice that leaves him wanting more explanation.

"Why?"

"Monsters can't live in cabinets, they're too small. We don't have any monsters around here and even if some do make a visit they won't come in here."

"Why?"

He stands up proudly and smiles without trying to, "Monsters are scared of blond hair." He walks over and runs his fingers through TJ's. "They know we are here and they stay away."

“Oh.” Ten little fingers pull the sheets back up a little. “Daddy?”

“Yes?”

“What about you?” As he got to the door Donovan Staples stopped cold as the words hit him and ran his hands through his own brown hair cut short just days ago.

“Don’t worry about me. Mommy will protect me.”

“Ok.” TJ nodded his head, Mommy would be there, that’s true. Without the thrill of the hunt his weary muscles pulled his eyelids shut for him.

Once the door was closed Donovan tip toed across the hall and opened another that looked just like it. As he put his left foot inside the room a woman’s voice whispered to him. “How is he doing?”

“I put him to bed.”

Her hair spilled all over his side of the bed, the very same color as his son’s, and the way it shines is an even more vivid image through the shadows. His eyes adjust to the lack of light and they frantically search for her face through all that hair. She’s almost as tightly packed into the bed as TJ was, with the sheets set up around her chin. Her thin lips move through the darkness, “I put him to bed a half hour ago. What was he doing?”

“He said he was looking for monsters.”

Her face is smaller then most which heightens the effect a change of facial expression brings. She looks suddenly off. “You guys need to change the movies you watch.”

Donovan shrugged. “I think he likes being afraid of monsters. He gets to put himself on alert for a mysterious force that could be anywhere. There’s adventure in a little bit of fear, especially for a kid. If you really want me too I’ll stop watching them with him but I think it’s fine.” She was sitting up now and watching him as he unbuttoned his shirt and put it in a green laundry basket next to the door.

His figure was not intimidating or breathtaking but not bad, and years of her eyes traveling it had helped her look even harder for the best parts. Before he met her he was boring and before she met him she was out of her mind, the match was perfect.

“Is your Dad still down there?”

“Yeah.”

“Maybe TJ heard his snoring and thought it was a monster. I’m sure that’s what they would sound like.” Her lips curled deceptively as if the words were the funniest pie ever delivered to someone’s face.

Donovan slid off his shorts and into pajama pants. He always slept in pajama pants. A few times early on in the relationship she had tried to convince him to just lay with her naked before and after sex but that was just too weird. Sleeping naked confines you to that room. Having pajama pants on means that if an angel comes in your bedroom, you're not showing it your genitals. He responded to her with laughter and a shake of his head to dismiss the comment.

She had to be right. Monsters had to be hiding in between the nasty sounds of an insomniac sleeping. The pained collapse of a man for twenty or thirty minutes at a time before he kicks right out of his false slumber and looks around, only to find that nothings changed. No one knows what retirement should be and no one knows what it is until they are in it. It has to be monsters that kick his nose and wake him up, not respecting the peaceful sleep he's worked a lifetime for. Nothing else makes sense.

"You know what your Dad should do now that he's retired?"

"What, honey?"

"Shave that weird Magnum PI 80's mustache."

He pulled the covers up and got in under them, throwing his arm around the woman who would protect him from the monsters without even trying. "I'm not going to stay up so you can make fun of my father. I'm going to bed."

She smiles and attacks his right cheek with six kisses all on different areas. It's a blitzkrieg of positive physical movement that he didn't altogether anticipate so his arms flail a bit at his sides. Eventually she finishes and when she does her head lands on his shoulder gently curling the rest of her body to his side.

"Your cousin is coming in tomorrow, right?" She throws the words over his shoulder far enough that they march with an army's determination up the side of his neck and into his ear.

"And her fiancé too. Dad says he's funny."

Her eyes beamed to him and even though most people who know Amy think she is so beautiful with makeup, at night when she takes it all off she's spellbinding. It's the cruelest prank she could ever play on the world, slapping on layers to cover up the brilliant contours. Donovan doesn't mind since he gets divine truth every night. He outlasts the mask and treasures the evening. She makes sleeping so much cooler than it used to be.

"We'll see. I've got high standards."

"I know." She pretended like she was going to slap him and he braced himself but they both snickered at the other one and fell back into the warmth of paid time off.

No one in that house ever dreams of monsters. They never have. I guess if the monsters ever do get up a head of steam and attack the grounds, certain parties are on the lookout.

Earning Tom's Secret

The door anticipated her reaction and closed its eyes, bracing for the impact. Sandra closed her eyes too and used all of her frustration, most of her anger, and a third of her vocal strength. She wanted everyone on the other side of the door to be very clear as to what she would not do. She did more then scream; what she did could not casually be called yelling.

"NO!!!"

On the other side of the door Irene was much more shaken up. She threw both hands in the air and jolted backward with eyes wide open like out of a dream. Suddenly she understood how hard this situation was and turned her head to catch the eyes of the most frightened man who had ever stood in her house. His short brown hair flopping stupidly atop his confused brain, sheltered from the world by an impenetrable skull. Irene couldn't help but regret bringing them here. They seemed like good people but crazy. Sometimes good crazy, sometimes bad and she knew Tom wasn't going to like that.

"You go in the living room...with Tom." She did the shooing hand motion that you give to a cat who made its way on the table and is sniffing slowly at your food. He reacted just as suddenly and was gone before he fully understood her statement.

Irene faced the door again trying to look and imagine her face.

"Sandra. He's left the room now."

Things were quiet for a few seconds

"Can I come in?"

No response was given but after eighteen seconds she heard the lock click open.

Irene looked down at her hand as it turned the knob and wondered when it lost the good sense to tremble with nervousness in situations like these.

Tom's face is the human version of a water beaten rock. You can see life leaving tracks all over him. Its partially because he never lets his lips smile so the tight grimace pushes out all the imperfections. Like every house guest to cross the doorway he didn't like Tom and was unhappy to be in a room alone with him.

He tip toed into the living room without drawing any attention to his entrance. The glow of the television coated Tom completely.

"She ok?" His lips didn't even move yet he talked. Evan stood in shock, even more frightened of him than of the fact that his wife had locked herself in the bathroom.

"Not sure. I hope so." He sat in the large comfortable chair but he didn't sit in comfort. He squirmed, subconsciously trying to get Tom to look at him or show human frustration with his antsy body language. Tom let the sound "mmmmm." Come from his throat and act as an answer while moving only slightly. His right hand raised with a jet black plastic remote clutched tightly and all of a sudden the TV was commanding all sound in the room. A very simple sounding fellow was bellowing out expressions like "Winning is about that extra effort" and "If you want to stop these guys your going to have to hit them in the mouth." Evan began to track his favorites. So far it was "He refuses to lose" which they said a lot, as if some professional football players were much more open and fascinated at the prospect of losing then the more straight forward old fashioned players. Losing began to sound like a new fangled bohemian concept that all the kids liked but not us.

For a while he let the silence happen, it was good to think about something else and he wasn't sure what Tom liked besides football. After a while he couldn't keep it going anymore. He felt like the conversational shut out was an indictment of him. Somehow he wasn't good enough to talk to Tom and so he had to suffer in silence. Was Tom mad at him for what he said to Sandra? Did he know it was a joke?

If Tom was a television character he was the father on the show Wonder Years. He did communicate but only in the most comfortable situations or when important things were on the line. Evan didn't know the personality type. He liked Irene a lot but so did everyone else. She had a way of infecting the air around her with her personality like she was signing seconds with her signature and it was beautiful handwriting.

She was in the bathroom now not just trying to be a friend but earn one. Before Tom she had too many friends to catch up with, free drinks at almost every bar and all she could do was tip well to let them know she appreciated it. She felt so appreciated, but that was years ago when the world loved her. Now its just Tom.

He was everything that she had never experienced before and when it was just them he would hold her in silence or whisper to her and over a ten year span she came to love having no one else in the room. The world could never love her as much as Tom did and no one else would understand. He didn't feel they needed to.

Irene spoke with her hands and pleaded the case for Evan while Sandra tore into her as if she was him. It was going to take time to strip her of all the layers encasing her real reaction.

Evan was going to finally say something. He wouldn't sit and stew in the shame of being ignored. "What team do you root for?"

Tom shrugged his shoulders.

Back to the silence. Evan hated him even more now. Who does that to someone who is your guest and trying to make cordial conversation about something you apparently love? Evan wished he had said "Which man's testicles are you staring at the hardest through that see through spandex? Any favorites?" When he didn't respond Evan would quickly toss in "They must all look pretty good then. I understand." Tom was old but mean looking and has huge hands that look like clown gloves are on them. Evan did not want to be knocked out by an old person and have to explain that to his friends. If Tom lost who does he have to explain it to? He doesn't even have friends.

Tom only had one friend, he married her. She hated football, basketball (other than college), baseball, tennis, golf, and Nascar. She always picked the worst movie rentals and would find two good parts in them and then as the credits rolled say "I thought it was ok."

Evan wasn't trying to think of anything but he couldn't help but come back to her. How could two people go from perfect to lost and hating the life in each others bodies so quickly and so much? Sandra came to gatherings like this and looked perfect. She made sure she was flawless and worked so hard at being relaxed she had no idea whether she was but one comment can change everything. It doesn't take that much. It didn't seem to make sense that one blurting of words in that particular configuration could set them back this drastically and in the company of others.

"You heard what I said at dinner. Was it that bad?"

He shrugged again.

"I mean..."

Tom interrupted and raised the same right hand with the remote control extending out of it. "Football!"

For a second Evan did quiet himself but then he realized the man was a maniac and insensitive to the point he should be addressed directly. "Look man I'm kind of stressed out right now ok?! I might need to talk to you and if you can just let my blabbering run instead of their blabbering you can still watch the game!"

Tom pushed out his bottom lip and hit the mute button.

"You guys have been married for a long time and I respect that. We just got married in October. I was hoping when your wife met mine at work they could become friends and you guys could let us know any kind of tricks you've learned to make things easier. I'm not just sad about what is going on I'm confused and I don't know how to make things better because I don't understand what I did. I'm sorry if I thought you'd be able to help."

Tom nodded. "If I tell you the secret will you let me watch football?"

"What secret?" He thought this was going to be Tom opening himself up and exposing some kind of personal situation he would never tell anyone but it could act as a fable with morals hidden under it. He was very incorrect.

"Everything has a secret. Football has a secret to winning. Marriage has a secret to winning."

Evan stopped squirming and just lay in the chair. "What is the secret?"

Tom opened his lips but barely, like he had too but he hated to do it.

"You have to be someone she is happy to be in the room with, ninety percent of the time."

Evan nodded.

"No you don't understand. If your that guy for her ninety percent of the time no doubt can come to her mind that your still the one. At the same time your not going to ever be able to agree with her and be nice to her all of the time. She is an idiot sometimes the same way you are so you need that ten percent to blow off steam and she can accept it...if she gets ninety. Now do you understand?"

Evan nodded like he needed to prove he grasped it.

The only time Tom's head moved his neck turned his head and his eyes looked to the bathroom. "You tried to go in there." Tom shakes his head like a wet bulldog. "Bad move."

"I've never seen her this mad before I didn't..."

"My wife will talk her down a little. Get her back to presentable. When she comes out you stand right next to her and as you speak to my wife and me you slip your arm around her softly and say well we really should be going and you leave."

"That's when the arguing starts."

"True. You should argue but be nice."

"How?"

"Don't think about it just be nice while your explaining how you disagree. If you're nice she will be nice back after a while."

"Wow. Thanks I guess I never took the time to think..."

Tom whipped his glance to Evan for the first time pointing to the screen with the forefinger of his left hand and adding a strong word to the movement "Football!"

Evan nodded and sank back in the chair. He was going to get another beer and wait for Sandra. Maybe give this football game a chance. Could be good.

www.ingramcontent.com/pod-product-compliance
Ingram Content Group UK Ltd.
Pitfield, Milton Keynes, MK11 3LW, UK
UKHW040557210726
13854UKWH00007B/1373

9 780557 701179